SIXTEEN SCANDALS

BY SOPHIE JORDAN

HOUGHTON MIFFLIN HARCOURT

BOSTON   NEW YORK

hmhbooks.com

The text was set in Fairfield LT Std.
Title page illustrations and hand-lettering by Em Roberts
Chapter opener illustrations and note hand-lettering by Andrea Miller
Cover and interior design by Andrea Miller

Library of Congress Cataloging-in-Publication Data is on file.
ISBN: 978-0-358-20621-7

Manufactured in the United States of America
DOC 10 9 8 7 6 5 4 3 2 1
4500822588

A proper young lady should speak only a fraction above a whisper, lest she be considered a shrill termagant and brand herself unmarriageable.

—Lady Druthers's Guide to
Perfect Deportment and Etiquette

There are far worse things than being deemed unmarriageable. Probably . . .

her. And now she would quite possibly perish by doing something utterly childish: disobeying her parents.

She flinched as a body landed inches away, a big man pinned beneath a woman. Straddling him, the woman slapped him over and over with her reticule. From his pained grunts, she must have had a brick in her bag.

Clinging to the table's base, Primrose rotated, still squatting, and shuffled to the other side. She didn't look down at herself to confirm that she had ruined the beautiful gown she had borrowed.

She'd done this to herself. It was her choice to slip from the safety of her house. The first step she had taken toward freedom in, well, ever.

She could not have known it would lead to this though.

She could not have known when she woke this morning to disappointment and frustration and vowed to take command of her fate that this would be the result.

She could not have known that the best night of her life would end here . . . with her crouched beneath a table on a dirty tavern room floor with an army battling at every side.

Nor could she have expected the mighty crack above her splitting the table into shards and exposing her to all of London around her.

Oh yes. She was definitely going to die here.

She was going to die here, crouched beneath a table on a dirty tavern room floor with bits and crumbs of food that predated the Magna Carta surrounding her.

Glass shattered nearby, and she flinched, shrinking into herself as tiny shards sprayed her and the pungent scent of sweat, ale, and wine soaked the air.

If this was to be it, then it was an ignominious end.

She had always imagined there would be more to her life. She had simply imagined there would be . . . more life.

A woman screamed nearby. Or quite possibly a man.

She clutched the pedestal base of the shoddy table, clinging to it as though it would save her from the chaos.

The irony was not lost on her.

She would die on her birthday, at the tender age of ten and six—on the day that was supposed to mark her entrée into the world, on the day she was supposed to put childish things behind

SIXTEEN SCANDALS

For Louisa Edwards . . . for being
so very good at so many things.

Chapter One

TWELVE HOURS EARLIER . . .

Primrose Ainsworth had trained all her life for this day.

This training included a long list of do's and don'ts. To be fair, there was an excessive amount of don'ts on her list, largely due to *Lady Druthers's Guide to Perfect Deportment and Etiquette,* the only book Primrose could claim to abhor. As a devoted reader, someone who considered books to be her closest companions, this was saying a great deal.

Alas, Mama valued Lady Druthers's guide as no other book. It was her bible, a mariner's compass that directed her through the rearing of her daughters.

Even before Primrose could read its pages, the book had been read to her. Then, once she knew her letters, her governess had been charged with regularly evaluating Primrose to make certain she had the book memorized. Hours of recitation. She could be ignorant of the Battle of Hastings and its significance to British history for all Mama cared. As long as Primrose knew that blasted guide to manners and other torments front to back, her mother was satisfied.

A true optimist, Primrose had always concentrated on the do's rather than the don'ts in those pages. On the things she *would* be permitted to do at ten and six: Staying up late and dressing in a manner not suitable for nine-year-old girls. No more loosely fitted frocks and plaited hair in ribbons.

Instead, she could wear her hair in an elegant coiffure, sip champagne, waltz with handsome gentlemen, and attend salons on topics of art, literature, and science. These were but a few of the liberties to be hers—or any lady's, really—once she came out in Society.

Finally, Prim would no longer be a child consigned to the nursery. No more sneaking out to spy on her older sisters through the balusters as they entertained friends and suitors.

As the youngest of four girls, Primrose always had an abundance to observe, but for the two years since Aster had entered Society, she had been alone in her observations. Not that Aster had ever been one to join her in her forays to spy on their sisters, but these last couple years were especially lonely for Prim in the Ainsworth household. She had been forced to watch and wait her turn, counting first the years, then months, weeks, and days. Like a prisoner stuck in Newgate, she'd counted down the time until her release.

Envy had climbed high in her chest whenever her sisters slipped cloaks over their lustrous gowns to venture out to the theater or a dinner or a ball. They dazzled her, and she'd marveled at the idea that one day it would be her turn.

One day she would be like them.

One day she would know such freedoms.

That day had arrived.

Finally, she would be seen.

At last, she could attend events with her sisters. She could stay out late and partake in all the diversions permitted adults. That would be celebration enough for her.

Prim hastened downstairs to breakfast, eager to see her mother and learn what plans were in place now that she was of suitable age.

Obviously, nothing special was planned for today or she would already know of it. She did not even care that her parents were not hosting a party or dinner in her honor. Prim knew better than to expect that, especially this close to Violet's long-anticipated wedding. Prim was fine with a quieter debut. Truly.

Her family was of moderate means. Papa often bemoaned how costly it was to bring up four daughters. She knew no grand coming-out ball was in her future. That was for members of the peerage and much too impractical for the Ainsworth family. Prim's sisters had not received any such fête to commemorate their birthdays, and she knew to expect the same.

Currently, her family's focus was on her sister's impending wedding, which would thankfully be over and done in a fortnight. For now, Prim's expectations were simple. She wanted to be included in all social gatherings her family attended—that meant accompanying her parents and sisters in the evenings. These were not far-fetched hopes. It was reasonable to believe she would be treated as an adult now.

She didn't even require a new wardrobe. She could fit into all of Violet's old gowns, as her sister was already wearing her wedding trousseau, confident her betrothed would outfit her in new gowns as soon as they were married. Redding was rich enough. Violet reminded everyone of that no fewer than 672 times a week.

When Prim entered the dining room, Mama was already seated at the table, eating and sipping her tea as she browsed the scandal rags beside her like she was Napoleon examining a map of Europe.

Primrose cleared her throat. "Ahem."

No response.

She tried again, declaring rather grandly, "Good morning."

Mama returned the greeting with a distracted murmur, not glancing up from the day's gossip holding her rapt attention.

Papa at least looked around the edges of his paper at her. "Good morning, poppet." He then went back to reading.

Primrose studied them both, her anticipation ebbing over their lackluster reaction to the sight of her. She waited several more moments.

"It's someone's birthday," she called out, hoping that would gain her acknowledgment.

Perhaps they merely sought to surprise her?

The silence stretched and she admitted to herself that it was unlikely given her parents were not demonstrative people and they lacked a sense of humor in general.

Mama finally spoke, not glancing up. "Of course, it is. We have not forgotten." She took a moment longer, her finger tracking the sentence she was reading. With a sigh, she lowered her paper, and began to generously lather jam onto her toast with single-minded focus.

"Happy birthday, poppet." Papa looked around the edges of his paper once more. It was recognition, lackluster though it may be.

Mama had not said the words, but Prim now doubted she would. Her mother was not the effusive sort. At least not very often. When her daughters received marriage proposals, then she became quite demonstrative.

Apparently this, the fifteenth day of June, was not to be remarked on in any special way. It was to be treated as an ordinary occasion.

Prim cleared her throat. "I know we haven't anything planned for today, but—"

"Correct," Mama said perfunctorily, stabbing her toast once in the air. "I warned you that we haven't the time or attention to devote to you right now."

Prim nodded. "Of course. Yes. I know that, but I had hoped that I might join you out this evening since I am now—"

"Not possible."

Primrose flinched. The quick denial felt like a slap. She looked back and forth between her parents, instructing herself to stay calm and not panic. Begging or crying or coming at her parents aggressively would reap nothing.

She moistened her lips and took a careful breath. "You promised when I turned ten and six—"

"Yes, well, you should not be such a selfish girl to fling that at me now," Mama snapped, looking up from her toast to level a hard stare on Primrose. "Have you any notion of the stress involved with arranging Violet's wedding whilst ushering Aster through the marriage mart?" She rubbed her fingers at the center of her forehead as if the very mention of these things caused her pain.

"And the coin involved," Papa intoned from behind his paper.

Mama continued as though he had not spoken. It was her modus operandi to ignore all mentions of money.

"Aster is in her third season with no offer in sight." She wagged three fingers in emphasis, her eyes bulging as though in physical pain. "How can you expect me to allow you to make your entrée into Society? To have two daughters on the marriage mart at the same time? I did that with Violet and Aster. Never again. No, thank you very much. 'Tis madness. I shall not repeat that mistake. You can wait another year."

"Another year?"

"At least."

She gasped. "At *least*?"

"Oh do stop parroting me, Primrose." Mama released another long-suffering sigh. "You grow tedious."

Prim moved on numb legs toward the dining table and sank down onto a seat. She did not bother fetching herself a plate. She ignored all the tempting smells beckoning from the sideboard. Her stomach rolled. She feared that if she attempted food right now, she would be ill. She began cautiously, knowing it benefited her not to annoy her mother. "You're saying I might have to wait more than a year before my coming-out in Society?"

"Yes, well, one can hope Aster will have a betrothal by this time next year." Mama began lathering her second slice of toast.

She did not even look up as she delivered this most disastrous news.

Papa was buried in his paper, but Primrose tried appealing to him nonetheless. "Papa?"

He turned a page.

"Papa?" she said more insistently.

"Primrose," Mama chided. "Mind your tone. A lady does not shout."

Prim resisted the urge to argue that she wasn't shouting. It would be for naught. That would only bring forth another reprimand. As far as Mama was concerned, anything above a whisper was considered excessive. Unless it was Mama doing the shouting, of course.

Papa lowered the paper with a mild grunt, peering at Prim and Mama blandly through his spectacles. "Yes, m'dears?"

"I'm ten and six, Papa. *Today*," she said, putting weight on the final word, hoping it would affect him in some way. She knew she could not reach her mother. Papa was her only hope. "Mama says I must wait to come out at least another year."

Prim held her breath, searching his face, hoping Papa might intervene on her behalf.

Mama took a crunchy bite of toast and spoke with great agitation through a mouthful, bits of crumbs flying from her lips. "Do not try to appeal to your father. It will do no good. He and I are in accord on this. I'll not have two daughters competing for suitors again. Aster is enough of an ordeal on her own." She shuddered and took another angry bite.

Primrose shook her head, bewildered. Most assuredly, Mama had made her mind up long ago. She had simply not seen fit to inform Prim. If only she had told Prim this months ago, weeks even, then she would not now face such crushing disappointment . . . and such a keen sense of betrayal at this moment.

Mama went on, "Once Aster is betrothed, you will then have your turn, Primrose."

Prim's shoulders slumped.

When her mother said it like that, it sounded so *annoyingly* reasonable.

Last born, last daughter remembered.

Mama choosing Aster over Prim was nothing out of the ordinary. Mama was always choosing one of her three elder daughters over Prim. It was the condition of her life.

Papa nodded. "A sound plan, Primrose. I am certain you see the sense in that. Once Aster is betrothed, you will have your mother's most dedicated attentions on you."

Truth be told, to be out in Society *without* Mama's full attention sounded like a blessing, but Prim dared not say that.

As she slumped in her chair, Aster and Violet entered the room and made their way to the sideboard, where breakfast awaited their selection.

Aster and Violet bore the same coloring, with their deep chestnut hair and milk-and-roses complexions, but there the similarity ended.

Violet was curvaceous and moved as gracefully as a floating snowflake. Many a suitor had written odes to her grace and beauty. She received no fewer than four proposals during her first season, and three in her second, but Violet had waited, claiming a bigger and better fish was coming. That fish had arrived in her third season in the form of Redding. She had finally accepted him, to Mama's great joy.

Contrariwise, Aster was somewhat boxlike. She did not float when she walked like Violet. Rather, she charged ahead with jarring steps as though in a rush to reach her destination. Mama once claimed she was shaped like a tree stump—this was after a frustrating morning spent at the dressmaker's when nothing poor Aster tried on appeased Mama.

Violet seated herself first.

Aster soon followed, her plate piled high with food, quite ready to enjoy her meal.

Mama frowned. "Aster, what have I said about daintier, lady-like portions?"

Aster shrugged and took a bite of her kipper with an almost defiant air. She didn't care. She enjoyed food and ate with gusto.

Prim sat in silence as the conversation moved from tonight's diversion to events beyond that, namely Violet's upcoming wedding.

"And what are your plans for the day, Primrose?" Mama asked, finally turning her attention back to her youngest daughter.

She looked up warily at the question, feeling as though she were facing a firing squad. The inquiry felt like a trap. Since Prim was not preparing for an evening out, she would be doing nothing extraordinary or particularly diverting. Mama must know that. She rarely inquired after Prim's day, as her options were obviously limited. Prim was not allowed to leave the house without a chaperone, after all.

Most girls not yet out in Society spent their days working

through their lessons with their governess. Occasionally they strolled the park or the halls of a museum. They had tutors, too, in dance or voice or pianoforte.

Not Primrose though.

Mama had deemed her *finished* over two years ago, around the time that Aster entered Society. Even though Prim could not carry a tune. Even though her skill at the pianoforte was abysmal.

Prim had been on her own for quite some time without a governess or tutor. There had been no dancing instructor, but Prim enjoyed dancing and was passable at it. Aster had no interest and made no effort to master her steps, so Violet had skipped right to Primrose to practice. For that reason alone, Primrose knew all the dances: the quadrille, the cotillion, and even the most scandalous waltz.

And yet, since Violet had become betrothed, she'd had little need for dance practice, so Prim's days were spent in rather dull occupation. If she did not have plans with Olympia, she usually engaged herself in reading.

"My plans?" she echoed.

"Yes. What do you have planned for your day?"

Prim swallowed. Dread worked a slow churn in her belly. "I have plans to meet Olympia at Gunter's. I thought I mentioned that last week."

She had *not* mentioned any such thing to her mother, but sometimes subterfuge worked. Mama was less than attentive when Prim spoke. Prim often claimed she'd gotten permission when she in fact had not. Fortunately for her, Mama could never remember.

Mama pursed her lips. It was her usual expression when Olympia's name entered any conversation.

As far as Mama was concerned, Olympia was ill-bred. Her mother was a performer—a word tantamount to *peasant* in Mama's mind. If Olympia's mother were not world renowned and fêted by all of London society, Mama would have forbidden their friendship from the start.

Approval aside, however reluctantly given, Mama looked as though she had sucked a lemon at the notion of Primrose taking tea at Gunter's with Olympia.

"I trust you can be chaperoned by her maid. Goodness knows they have more staff than they require. Your sisters and I are venturing to Bond Street and we shall have need of Gertie."

Of course Prim was not included in their shopping trip. Not even on her birthday, when Mama might make a special treat out of it for her.

"I am certain one of Olympia's maids will accompany us," Prim assured her mother, determined to keep her outing with her friend.

Papa lowered his paper with a scowl. He was no doubt alarmed at the mention of Bond Street, the location of the finest and most popular shops in London. If Mama required two servants, there would be quite a few packages to carry.

"Bond Street?" Papa's tone conveyed his concern.

"Now, now. Do not look at me that way, my dear Mr. Ainsworth. You haven't any notion of how difficult it is to keep two daughters properly outfitted for the height of the season." She wagged two fingers in the air as though the gesture were necessary for emphasis. "Aster is yet unwed and in dire need

11

of a suitor, and you know what a challenge she is. She never likes anything that is in vogue. I think she'd be happier wearing a burlap sack than one of Madame Brigitte's splendid creations."

Aster paused as she was delicately cracking at a soft-boiled egg with her spoon. "I am right here, Mama," she pointed out wryly, her gaze lifting from beneath her arched eyebrows.

Mama continued addressing Papa as though she had not spoken. "However will she ensnare an eligible gentleman if she's not adequately attired? Count your blessings Begonia is at least wed already." She sighed heartily.

"*I* am betrothed, Mama," Violet loftily reminded her as she nibbled at a piece of fruit. "You needn't outfit me for much longer. In a fortnight, I shall have all the dresses I desire. Redding has accounts at all the very best shops in town. I shall never want for anything." *Reminder 541 this week.* Prim and Aster locked eyes across the table and shared a knowing smirk.

Mama nodded and took another bite, speaking around a mouthful. "Indeed, my dear. You have far outshone Begonia. You are a credit to our family with the fine match you have made."

Aster swung her spoon too hard then, loudly cracking her soft-boiled egg and sending shards of shell inside the tasty goodness.

Prim shook her head ruefully. Mama's remarks had ceased to surprise.

"But, oh!" Mama sank back against her chair and fanned herself with her napkin. "A wedding in a fortnight. I'm all agitation."

12

Primrose and Aster exchanged looks. Aster rolled her eyes in dramatic fashion.

"Aster," Violet added, "You can have all my old dresses as I will have so many new ones. Of course, you shall have to let out all the stays to fit you."

Aster's eyes shot daggers. "Are you certain you want to give me *all* your dresses, Violet? You may need them. You know how the servants talk . . . I overheard that your clever Redding is all thumbs and cannot quite manage to undo his buttons. He's constantly rending them and ruining his garments. You cannot be certain he won't reduce your gowns to shreds on your wedding night."

Violet slammed a hand on the table, rattling the dishes. "What rubbish! Redding can undo buttons! You're trying to nettle me with these fabrications."

Aster shrugged as though she could possibly be lying. She was expert at aggravating Violet, after all. Prim did not put it past her to fabricate something merely to irritate Violet.

"Aster, enough," Mama chided and then reached for her smelling salts. "I vow, you girls will put me in an early grave." She took a deep sniff, and then settled back in her chair, seemingly revived.

Papa harrumphed, rustling his paper. "You do understand we are expected to provide dowries for these gels?" Clearly, he was still stuck on the subject of their impending trip to Bond Street. "Dowries for the *three* we have left? Violet's might have already been negotiated, but I haven't had to pay it yet." He swept a hand encompassing Aster, Violet, and Primrose. "Consider that

13

as you are loading packages upon Gertie during your shopping expedition today." With a rattle of his paper, he returned his attention to the day's news.

As much as Papa disapproved of their shopping jaunt, Prim knew Gertie, a woman hired years ago to be the family governess, would not look forward to it more. Gertie's governess days were over. At least in the Ainsworth household.

Gertie had ushered all four of them through lessons in Latin, French, literature, mathematics, science, history, geography, and basic comportment. Oh, and rudimentary dance, as Papa refused to pay for a dancing instructor.

That was, until two years ago. A few days prior to Prim's fourteenth birthday, Gertie announced that she had reached the limits of her knowledge and could no longer properly instruct Primrose.

When she explained this to Prim's parents, instead of acquiring a new governess to meet Prim's needs, Mama declared her formal education at an end. After all, Prim had been successfully tutored in all matters of significance as far as Mama and Papa were concerned.

No one wants a wife too clever. Mama had been quick to offer that opinion then and several times since. Besides . . . she had such significant plans for Prim's older sisters marrying well, she did not see the need to squander money on Prim.

"Mama?" Violet frowned as though suddenly struck with a thought. "Are you certain Gertie will be enough help?"

Mama had kept Gertie on to serve as a lady's maid and companion among them. The former governess now helped with their hair and dress, served as a chaperone, and generally ran whatever errands Mama required.

"Perhaps we should drag Cook from the kitchens to carry packages, too?" Aster grumbled.

Violet glared at Aster across the table.

Aster smiled sweetly. "Is something amiss, *Violent?*"

Primrose lowered her head to hide her smile. Aster loved to warp Violet's name, and Prim found it vastly entertaining.

"Aster," Mama reprimanded, "Stop that. You know your sister's name." She held a finger aloft. "But you do pose a valid question. Is Gertie enough?" Her gaze narrowed in contemplation. "Perhaps we should bring a groom too."

Primrose set her napkin on the table and pushed up to her feet. She wasn't needed here. "If you'll excuse me."

Mama gave a distracted nod, her attention on Aster and Violet as she continued to strategize their shopping venture.

Prim had almost reached the doors when her mother's voice stopped her. "Oh, and you can plan to dine with Gertie this evening. We will all be at Mrs. Simeon's soirée and her affairs always run long. She hosts the most brilliant occasions though. No need to wait up for us."

They would be out and Primrose left home alone. No surprise there.

"That old windbag?" Aster muttered.

"Aster!" Mama chided. "Mrs. Simeon has great influence. All the most eligible gentlemen attend her functions, and you should take heed of her. One word of endorsement from her can go very far for a young lady."

Prim lingered. She could not help herself. *Ton* gossip did intrigue her. Anything that had to do with the world outside this house interested her. Naturally. She wasn't immune to High Society's gossip.

Papa peered around his paper. "Is my presence really required? Might I not dine with Gertie, too?"

"Mr. Ainsworth! Mrs. Simeon is cousin to the Dowager Duchess of Hampstead." Mama practically quivered with indignation.

"And what does that have to do with *my* attendance at tonight's soirée, m'dear?"

"You never know when the dowager duchess might appear at one of Mrs. Simeon's fêtes."

"The old dame has not graced any of Mrs. Simeon's parties with her presence yet," Aster reminded them as she cut into a juicy kipper, her ruined soft-boiled egg pushed to the side. "They might be blood kin, but apparently that does not obligate her to attend her cousin's gatherings. Heaven knows I would not be inclined to attend of any of Violet's."

"Good," Violet retorted. "Because I shan't invite you."

"Girls, stop your bickering." Mama glared at Aster, clearly unappreciative of her input. "You never know when yet the dowager will show—or even better—when her son, the young Duke of Hampstead, might make an appearance."

"Young Hampstead eschews all polite Society," Violet announced with an air of authority. Ever since her betrothal to Redding, she had turned into an expert on all matters of Society. "Everyone knows he has a small set of friends and prefers them to ballrooms."

"One day he shall give that up. He will need to wed and produce an heir."

"I've seen this young duke at my club," Papa commented mildly through the barrier of his paper.

Mama gaped. "Mr. Ainsworth! You've never said as such. What is he like?"

"He's a bit of a wild buck," Papa mused as he turned his paper to the next page.

Mama looked almost affronted at the remark. "He's young, only but ten and nine, I believe. Newly minted. That's to be expected. He *is* the most eligible nobleman in the realm. Handsome and rich as Croesus."

"Is it no wonder he spends so little time at the *ton*'s approved venues, with all you marriage-minded mamas slavering after him."

It was a bit of irony, Primrose supposed, thinking of this unknown, faceless duke. She wanted so desperately to be seen and treated as an adult—to be let out of the nursery, for goodness sake—whilst this duke, this man, a mere *lad*, from all accounts, not so very much older than herself, had all the freedom in the world. He had wealth and opportunity. Every door was open to him, and he chose not to cross the threshold of any of them.

She didn't even know him, but she hated him a little.

"The lad has to marry someday and he has no need of a dowry. He can wed whomever he wants. So why not one of our . . ." Mama's voice faded as she alternated her gaze on Aster and then Primrose. Whatever she saw in the two of them made the excitement dim from her eyes. Her shoulders slumped in defeat. "That's neither here nor there, I suppose."

The insult was thinly veiled, and Primrose saw right through it. As far as Mama was concerned, the two most attractive Ainsworth daughters had already been matched. Mama did not expect the less appealing two to fare better.

Mama resumed with a beleaguered sigh. "In any event, it is quite a coup to be invited to Mrs. Simeon's events. We are among the privileged chosen."

Except for Primrose. She was not chosen. Even today, on her birthday. The vast unfairness of it all weighed down on her and pushed her to move.

Snapping back to action, she departed the room, glad to leave them to talk about all the things they would do without her.

Once in her bedchamber, she checked her reflection in her cheval mirror, looking herself over carefully. She pinched her cheeks for a bit of color. Cringing at the hopeless sight of her hair, she attempted to smooth down the tendrils that sprang from her coronet of plaits. Her hair was perpetually untidy. It would take more time than she had to tame the fiery strands.

She paced the length of her chamber, biding her time as patiently as she could until she needed to leave for her meeting with Olympia. A challenging task. Patience was the least of her virtues.

When she could wait no longer, she snatched up her reticule and fled her room.

In the foyer, she grabbed her bonnet and arranged it on her head. *There.* That would hide her less-than-perfect hair. She turned in a small circle, as though expecting to see someone in the entrance hall to bid her farewell, to inquire when she might return. Her mother or her father. Her sisters. Gertie or the housekeeper.

No one was about. She turned for the door. No one made note of her leaving the house, which wasn't as much of a surprise as it should have been.

She was the forgotten daughter, after all. Mama might keep tabs on her, but that was only superficially. Invisibility was the proven condition of her life.

~~Know your place in the social hierarchy.~~
~~There is nothing so gauche as a lady who looks~~
~~high above herself—except the one who lowers~~
~~herself beneath the station to which she was born.~~

—Lady Druthers's Guide to
Perfect Deportment and Etiquette

The youngest daughter
always comes last.

Chapter Two

It was a rare sunny day as Primrose emerged from her house. Not a cloud in the sky. Perfect summer weather. She looked both ways for any carriages before crossing the street to Olympia's house.

The Zaher's housekeeper opened the door promptly at Prim's knock, a smile quick to form on her lips.

All of Olympia's household staff wore friendly expressions. Prim knew they had to be happier with their situation than the Ainsworth staff. Her household servants, few as they were, looked chronically tense, as though calamity could strike at any time. Because it often did. Certainly the Zaher staff was paid a better wage. That, too, likely made a difference.

Mama and Prim's sisters (excepting Aster) had a penchant for histrionics. Aster undoubtedly enjoyed causing said histrionics. She had a knack for needling Violet and, once upon a time, Begonia. Of course, Aster's unflappable nature amidst chaos annoyed Violet and Begonia to no end. Whether it was the news that a particularly favored bachelor had been lost to a rival debutante or the tragedy of a misplaced hair comb, such catastrophes could result in calamitous wails. And there was Aster, smiling suspiciously amid it all, so that Primrose had a strong notion of who'd hidden the hair comb.

"Well, happy tidings to you, Miss Primrose. And how are you on this fine day?" The housekeeper leaned forward with a sweet grin. "I understand someone is a year older."

She resisted pointing out that she happened to be only a day older than yesterday. "Thank you, Mrs. Davis. Yes, it is my birthday."

"Splendid. Happy birthday. I thought you were meeting Miss Olympia and Mrs. Zaher at Gunter's? They left early this morning for the theater. Mrs. Zaher had some business to attend to there first."

"Yes, the plan was to meet them there, but my mother and sisters have need of Gertie, who was to accompany me."

She knew that Mrs. Zaher had a dress rehearsal this morning and Olympia had joined her. Prim envied the interesting things Olympia did courtesy of her mother. Not only was she allowed to attend her mother's performances, but she joined her at many salons throughout Town where Mrs. Zaher was a featured guest. All kinds of artists and eccentrics frequented these salons. People Prim would never have an opportunity to meet in her family's very modest and conventional circles.

"Oh dear." Mrs. Davis clasped her hands together.

Prim turned over the notion of walking to Gunter's all by herself, unescorted. It was unseemly behavior, to be certain, but it *was* her birthday. Even if her family did not think it deserved to be marked in any special manner, she wanted to do something to celebrate. And that did not mean returning home.

Mama might have decided to brush the day away as one might swipe lint off a sleeve. But Prim would not waste the day indoors with only her own company to entertain herself. Indeed not. She owed it to herself to mark the day in some fashion. Besides. It was not as though she never bent the rules of propriety. She did when it suited her — or when she was desperate enough.

Mrs. Davis snapped her fingers. "I have it. You can take one of the carriages. I'll have our coachman, John, deposit you directly at the shop's door."

"Oh I could not dare to impose —"

"Rubbish. I insist. And I know Mrs. Zaher and Miss Olympia would too." The housekeeper's eyes adopted a decided glint. "It is your birthday, after all."

Prim opened her mouth to further protest and then stopped herself.

Why not?

Why should she not accept?

"Very well," she agreed. "Thank you."

Mrs. Davis beamed and gestured ahead of her. "This way."

She followed the housekeeper through the door, her gaze immediately going to the elegantly papered walls. It was a much more fashionable arrangement than her own home's, richly and finely appointed with art and furniture and bric-a-brac. A large vase of fresh flowers sat on a table in the entry hall. Primrose knew for a fact it was changed out every few days. Mrs. Zaher loved her fresh flowers. Even in the winter months she had them brought in from hothouses.

It mattered naught that Mrs. Zaher earned every farthing through her considerable talents. She labored for the roof over their heads, for their smart dresses, for the baubles that far outshone anything Prim or her sisters possessed.

Mama was not impressed by any of it because of who Mrs. Zaher was.

Mrs. Zaher performed before audiences for coin. Considerable coin or not, such activity was forever a blemish against her in Mama's eyes. Mama maintained that gentlewomen did not labor for their livelihoods—not any more than gentlemen should—to do so was common as far as Mama was concerned.

Only Mrs. Zaher's renown and popularity and connections kept Mama's disdain in check. Without Mama's small-minded ways, Prim would not be allowed to be friends with Olympia.

A strange twist of conditions, but there it was. Of course Mama was ridiculous and shallow—all traits Prim abhorred—but Mama's inability to overlook Mrs. Zaher's popularity among the *ton* worked in Prim's favor. For no other reason would Mama have permitted Primrose to spend time with Olympia. Mama was forever harping on the fact that Mrs. Zaher was a woman, a widow, and a foreigner, in addition to daring to toil in the lowly arts.

Once safely ensconced in the Zaher's carriage, Prim settled against the luxurious velvet squabs for the short ride to the popular teashop.

Berkley Square was crowded as usual and it took some careful maneuvering for the coachman to take Prim as close as possible to the door of the shop. Once the vehicle had stopped, she waited anxiously for the carriage door to open and a doorman to hand her down.

Prim called a quick thank-you to the coachman and faced the shop, where Olympia and her mother likely already waited inside.

Primrose was mistaken.

Prim stood in the threshold, clutching her reticule close, scanning the shop and trying not to feel awkward in her aloneness, but it appeared they had not arrived.

Almost every table was occupied with very fashionable people, as always. Of course, Gunter's catered only to those privileged enough to splurge coin on ices and cakes and sweet biscuits. Prim had been to the shop a few times before with Olympia, never with her own mother and sisters though. It was a place where one might see and be seen. One of the very few places a young girl who was not officially out in Society could frequent.

Feeling the stares of those intimidatingly fashionable people on her now, Prim moved out of the threshold and to a side wall. Leaning against it, she hoped that she, an unaccompanied lady, might attract less notice in this new position. As willing as she was to bend the rules, she knew arriving here unescorted was simply not done for a young lady. More importantly, it was exceedingly awkward. Her heart pounded painfully in her chest as she waited, wishing now that she had been late.

Fortunately, she did not see anyone she knew. The last thing she needed was word getting back to Mama that her youngest daughter was spotted at Gunter's *alone*.

A bell jingled at the door as new customers entered.

It was a trio of well-dressed gentlemen. Prim could glimpse only their profiles, then the backs of their heads as they advanced into the shop, moving past her without a glance her way.

They carried themselves with the confidence and assurance of male entitlement. They were gentry. She surmised that at once from the boldness of their strides and the raucous nature of their voices and laughter. The fine cut of their clothing, if not their bearing, proclaimed these young bucks to be good *ton*.

They were just short of disruptive. Not that anyone would dare take them to task if they actually crossed that line. Everyone gawked at them and whispered indiscreetly as they took their seats at a table. Prim resisted the urge to roll her eyes.

She glanced around at those ogling faces in bemusement until it occurred to her that the men were being stared at unusually long and rather intensely. No one was looking at her anymore, as all the attention was riveted on the newcomers.

They must be more than good *ton*.

They were most certainly gentry. At the very least.

Perhaps one or more of them was even peerage. *Nobility*.

She studied them curiously. They talked and laughed among themselves, unaware or indifferent to the attention they garnered. A server approached and took their orders.

The table directly to Prim's right became empty and she slid into a chair, hoping to appear as inconspicuous as possible until Olympia and her mother arrived.

She was grateful for the gentlemen's presence. Not only did it distract from the social gaffe of a solitary lady occupying a table at Gunter's, but it gave her ample opportunity to study the nobs like everyone else in the shop.

Prim's gaze paused on the young man seated at the center of the trio.

He was extraordinary.

Granted, she did not have a great deal of exposure to young gentlemen, tucked away and hidden from Society such as she was, but she'd had her share of strolls in the park, occasional shopping trips, and socializing with extended family and her sisters' suitors. Amid all that, she had never seen anything close to the masculine perfection of this man.

Man was a loose designation. He appeared a few years older than she, and yet nothing about him proclaimed *boy*. His warm brown eyes gleamed with the intelligence and wit reserved for one who had done a fair share of living.

Perhaps he entered life with this quality and it had naught to do with the substance of his years. Perhaps he was born looking out at the world with wise eyes. Eyes set in an altogether pleasing face. Square-jawed. Noble brow. Aquiline nose.

He smiled at something one of his companions said, and she was rewarded with a flash of straight white teeth. That smile was devastating. It had a charming crookedness to it—a lopsided quality that belied his serious and intense face.

Prim inhaled a bewildered breath.

She'd never been so affected at the sight of another person. Her pulse hammered against her throat. He was a beautiful creature, almost too handsome to be real. Perhaps this was what Phoebe meant in Shakespeare's *As You Like It*: "Whoever loved that loved not at first sight"?

Prim gave a swift shake of her head to clear it of the ridiculous notion. She might very well be a dreamer—Mama had laid that accusation at her feet often enough—but she had never felt so *absurd* as she did in this moment.

Love at first sight was illogical. It did not exist.

Prim's trance was thankfully broken as the bell over the door jingled someone's entry.

Olympia and Mrs. Zaher breezed into the shop on a gust of summer-laced wind.

There was nothing inconspicuous about them. They dressed in the height of fashion. Unlike Mama, Mrs. Zaher did not subscribe to the unyielding notion that unmarried ladies should wear only white and pastels, leaving the bold colors for married women past the first blush of youth and well established within Society. Olympia's mother never forced her into the pastels Prim was made to wear. Nay, nothing borrowed or out of season ever graced Olympia's flawless skin. In all the years Prim had known Olympia, she had never seen her with a blemish, so unlike herself, whose freckled, finnicky skin was always on the verge of breaking out with a new spot at the slightest exposure to sunlight.

Olympia's perfection was no less striking today. She was presently outfitted in a walking dress of deep cobalt. The fabric was stunning against her light brown skin and midnight hair—hair that was manipulated into an elegant chignon with charming curls surrounding her face, all arranged by the Parisian hairdresser Mrs. Zaher kept on staff.

It was easy to feel jealous of her friend. That didn't mean she loved her less. Olympia was beautiful and kind and had a mother keen on exposing her daughter to all manner of adventures. Sometimes Prim wondered why Olympia even wanted her for a friend. By comparison, Primrose was so very . . . limited. She could go nowhere, do nothing save take strolls, stare out windows, and occasionally sneak away for an outing together. She often worried that one day Olympia would decide their friendship was too much trouble and not nearly rewarding enough to continue.

Olympia carried a large bunch of flowers in her arms. "For you, dear girl, a birthday bouquet to commemorate your special day. So very sorry to have kept you waiting. I hope you weren't here long." Olympia bestowed the bouquet with a great flourish.

Primrose blinked, her gaze suddenly watering as she admired the riotous profusion of poppies and primroses. "They are beautiful," she murmured, reaching down to stroke a petal. Prim looked up at her beloved friend and Mrs. Zaher, who smiled back fondly. It was touching how much they cared for her.

Prim's own family had treated this momentous birthday as an afterthought. She pushed that thought away. Things could always be worse. So Prim's family was not perfect. She knew that. What family was? To mourn that fact felt pointless.

Prim had a roof over her head, a warm bed at night, food in her belly, and she never feared harm. Such was her solace. She knew this world was not kind to those without the protection of good family—and in particular to women without men of some influence and financial stability to provide security. There were workhouses. Foundling homes. As terrible and unsavory as those fates could be, she knew even worse existed beyond that. Terrible, unspeakable things.

Olympia sank down in the chair beside her. "What is this morose face?"

Primrose blinked and schooled her features into a properly pleasant expression. "I was worried you weren't coming."

"The florist had a longer line than expected." Olympia clapped her hands together and rubbed them gleefully. "Now, what is it to be? Where and when will you be making your grand debut? Has your mother decided what you can do first?"

A server approached the table to take their order. Mrs. Zaher crisply removed her gloves with elegant movements and ordered tea for the table. Her gaze swept over Olympia and Primrose. "Shall we have some scones before you girls indulge in your ices? It's a special day, after all. We should have anything and everything we want." Her dark eyes glittered with merriment as she turned her attention to their server to inquire about the various pastry options in her dulcet voice.

Prim took advantage of her distraction. It was rather embarrassing to admit her mother's failings when Mrs. Zaher was a mother who lovingly pampered her daughter and lavished her with attention.

Prim leaned toward Olympia. "There will be no marking of this day, I fear," she confessed.

Olympia released a puff of laughter as though Prim had just made a jest. "Well, certainly there will be *some* recognition given of your birthday. You're now allowed out into Society. What shall you do first?"

"Oh. Um. Something." She winced at the vagueness of her response. "Next year. Hopefully," she replied with a small, unavoidable amount of rancor. Her indignation still bubbled very close to the surface. It was impossible to keep out of her voice. "Maybe." *If* Aster was betrothed by this time next year— something she appeared in no hurry to do.

Mrs. Zaher finished ordering and Prim felt the return of her attention keenly.

"So you will not have even a small party in your honor?" Olympia pressed. "Nothing at all?"

Prim nodded. "Correct." Another nod. "There will be no party. No dinner."

Olympia digested that. "Not even a tea? No special outing? You will not go . . . *anywhere?*"

"Nothing," she confirmed again.

"Olympia," Mrs. Zaher said softly, reaching for her daughter's hand and giving it a telling squeeze.

"Oh." Olympia blinked several times in rapid succession. The single word fell heavily between the three of them. "I see."

"Good." Prim was relieved she did not have to keep explaining.

"You will simply slide into Society alongside Aster." Olympia fixed a forced, overly bright smile on her face. "It will be fine. Isn't your family attending the theater on Tuesday? You can—"

"I'm not even to be granted that. I am not permitted out. Yet."

Olympia's smile slipped. "What do you mean? You're still consigned to the nursery like a—a *child?*"

Apparently Prim was not finished explaining.

"Until Aster becomes betrothed. Mama does not wish to usher both of us through the season at once. Evidently two daughters on the marriage mart is not to be endured." She fought the urge to roll her eyes. Mama insisted such a habit was vulgar behavior.

"She only now informed you of this?"

Prim shrugged. "She informed me this morning when I came down to breakfast that my entrée into Society would be delayed." She shook her head. "I should have expected as much."

"Expect?" Olympia scoffed. "You are now ten and six. You are in a position to *expect* things, Prim. You are in a position to demand—"

"No." Primrose took a ragged breath and shrugged. "I'm in no position to demand anything of my mother. You know that. I'm at the bottom of the hierarchy in my family. I cannot expect . . ." Prim trailed off.

It was not self-pity speaking. It was not defeat. Prim liked to think of it as pragmatism. If she wanted something badly enough, it was up to her to get it for herself. She had long ago realized that. If Mama denied her, she simply went around her.

Ever since she was a little girl, if Mama said no more biscuits, Prim merely stuffed them in her mouth when she wasn't looking. If Mama said no to a walk in the park, Prim would wait, bide her time, and slip out during Mama's afternoon nap. When Mama insisted she was finished with her education, Prim would claim she was making a social call to Olympia and instead visit one of London's well-stocked bookshops. There, she would use what little pin money she possessed to acquire new books, at times trading some of her own well-read ones with the proprietor. A difficult thing always, deciding which books to part with, but she would not have new books to read otherwise. Sacrifices had to be made for the improvement of her mind . . . and to stave off boredom. There were days she was convinced she would perish from lack of stimulation.

Mama called her defiant. Difficult. Hoydenish.

Perhaps.

Prim was all about circumventing her parents to get the things she wanted. Nothing too radical or outrageous, of course. She wasn't that brave or bold or foolish. These were merely little rebellions to help maintain her sanity. If she did not at times defy her parents, she feared she would shrivel up inside and die.

"I don't understand how you can tolerate such a situation. It's your blasted birthday!"

Prim twisted her shoulder in an awkward shrug. It wasn't the first time Olympia had voiced criticism over the way Prim's family treated her, and she never knew how to respond.

Mrs. Zaher tsked her tongue, the sound rife with disapproval. "Olympia, dearest. Don't persuade Primrose to go against her family."

"Of course, Mam," she said humbly. Her friend was all fire and boldness, except when it came to her mother. Olympia doted on her and never went against her. And why should she? There was no need for rebellion when one had their way in almost everything.

"That's a good girl." Mrs. Zaher's face brightened as their tea and scones arrived, and once again Olympia took advantage of her mother's inattention to shake her head violently *no* at Prim. Then she mouthed words Prim could not entirely decipher. She said either: "Your mum can stuff it" or "I like rum buckets."

Primrose grinned and shook her head at her irreverent friend. She certainly made the drudgery of life bearable. It was in the midst of admiring her audacious friend that her gaze cut again to the man-boy seated across from them. How could she not sneak another look at him? If for no other reason than to assure herself that he was real and not a figment of her imagination.

Only now her scrutiny was not unnoted. Indeed. It was returned in full, stunning measure.

Prim froze, looking at him looking at *her* with those deep brown, too-shrewd eyes of his.

He was looking at her. Not over her. Not around her. Not through her. *At her.*

That was a wholly new sensation—to find herself the center of such avid attention.

She felt his gaze touch her everywhere, as palpable as the stroke of a hand: from her unfortunate carroty-red hair and spotted nose, which her mother despaired of, to the profusion of flowers cradled in her lap.

The three gentlemen rose from their table, finished and ready to depart.

They came abreast of where Prim sat with Olympia and Mrs. Zaher.

Man-boy, as she had dubbed him in her mind, still watched her closely.

Her cheeks flushed hot. She should tear her gaze away from him. It wasn't appropriate. She should be blind to it—to *him*— and not be thinking of foolish Shakespeare lines. Ladies did not hold prolonged stares with strange gentleman. Even if they were handsome. Even if they were very likely peerage.

She should feign ignorance of his regard.

Except she could not. That would require steelier resolve than she possessed.

Suddenly, man-boy paused, stopping directly beside her table. His friends moved on ahead, but he lingered, unbelievable and awkward as that was.

He inclined his head politely to each of them, murmuring, "Good day, ladies." To Olympia's mother, he added, "Mrs. Zaher. I heard you sing at Haymarket. Allow me to say, your performance was inspirational."

"Thank you." Mrs. Zaher inclined her head, regal as a queen. She was accustomed to such lavish praise. "You're too kind." Accustomed to it, but still gracious.

His gaze returned to Prim again. "And happy birthday to you, miss."

She blinked. He was speaking to her.

He wished her happy birthday . . . which was more than her own family members had done today. She blinked again, struggling to find her voice and not appear a tongue-tied ninny.

With a nod, she finally mumbled something that might have been a thank-you. She was not sure. She could not be certain. Her mind was awhirl.

Then, with a polite inclination of his head, he was gone.

The door rang out at his departure.

"Well," Mrs. Zaher exclaimed. "Isn't he a handsome lad? Such lovely teeth."

"Who is he?" Prim murmured, stretching her neck and still staring at the door as though he might return.

Mrs. Zaher amended, "I suppose it's not very correct of me to call him a *lad*. He is clearly of age."

Olympia lifted a scone to her lips. "Agreed. He's like no lad I've ever seen."

"Who is he?" Primrose asked again.

Olympia answered, "No idea, but he's clearly Quality."

Clearly. And he spoke to her. To Primrose.

He had wished her a happy birthday.

Her mother would likely lift both eyebrows to the sky in disbelief if she knew that Primrose had been singled out by a Gentleman of Quality. A gentleman who was very likely a peer.

Violet and Begonia were considered the beauties. Mama did not have much faith in Aster or Primrose to charm anyone. Still, she would savor the memory of this exchange. Whether he was charmed by her or not—the memory of his deep voice wishing her happy birthday reverberated through her mind and made her feel warm and fuzzy inside.

Until she realized it would be the last time she heard that voice.

The last time he would ever speak to her.

The last time *any* handsome and exciting young man would likely *ever* speak to her if Prim looked to her sisters as examples of what to expect once she entered Society. Mama would watch her like a hawk. There would be no conversing or flirting with gentlemen of Prim's choosing. Potential suitors would all be curated by Mama, and would all be perfectly dull, no thought given to age or attractiveness, just the depth of their pockets.

Prim's shoulders slumped. The warm fuzziness faded, replaced by a tangled ball of knots in her stomach.

Even once she entered Society, she and the man-boy with alluring eyes and perfect teeth would likely never cross paths again. They moved in different circles. She could tell that at once from his manner and the company he kept. Unless she spotted him strolling on the street or in the park, he would be in his world and Prim would be in hers—a world regulated by her mother.

She pushed aside the unaccountable disappointment, determined to enjoy her outing with Olympia.

They finished their tea and scones amid happy chatter. Even full as they were, they ordered ices. Primrose managed to take down every last spoonful of the melon-flavored deliciousness.

As they left their seats, a new realization seized Prim—well, not new precisely—simply something she had not fully absorbed until this moment.

Not only would she not have another exchange with handsome young men in tea shops—but once Aster was betrothed, Mama would turn all her attention to marrying off Prim.

All her considerable and exhausting attention.

She might not be on the receiving end of that attention now, but her turn would come. For the first time, a frisson of dread skittered down her spine at the notion of entering Society. She'd only ever thought of the opportunity to do more, to see more, to seize the freedom that awaited her.

When Mama turned her most determined attention on Prim, there would be no stopping her. No reprieve. She'd seen Mama run roughshod over her sisters. She controlled everything: how they wore their hair, how they dressed, what invitations they accepted, which parties they attended, which gentlemen could pay court to them.

Prim's oldest sister had now been married for six years to a man twenty-two years her senior. They already had three children, all girls, and her sister was increasing with their fourth child. Begonia never looked happy. She did not look sad either. She simply looked exhausted. Tired and dead eyed.

Violet, inversely, looked delighted. She glowed like a child offered a present. Her betrothed was closer in age to her and the son of a man who owned a large mill in Farnham. The family was wealthy, and growing richer by the day on the sweat of laborers. Violet did not seem too troubled at that. Just as she did not seem to mind that he had an obnoxious laugh, picked his teeth with his dinner knife, and had expressly stated that women should not be educated for fear it would be too arduous for their weak minds. Ironic, that, considering he had never impressed Primrose with his intellect.

Mama was after her own comfort, of course. She had forgotten her usual snobbery and turned a blind eye to the fact that Redding's family was in trade and capitalizing on what was little better than indentured labor. They were rich and there would be vacations to the Cotswolds for all.

It was no secret that Mama was determined to elevate her status through her daughters. That had been her goal in securing matches for Begonia and Violet. It was her goal for Aster, too. And it would be her goal for Primrose. Mama was predictable in that manner.

Prim let these thoughts roll through her mind on the carriage ride home. She stared out the window with her bouquet nestled in her lap, lost in her musings, wondering how she might avoid Begonia's unfortunate fate.

The carriage rolled to a stop. "We're here," Olympia announced. "Would you like to come inside?"

Prim nodded. "Yes, thank you." There was no rush getting home, after all. No one was waiting for her.

She listened with half an ear as her friend chatted on the way into the drawing room.

Prim's thoughts churned. She had a year. Perhaps longer if Aster dragged her feet, as, of course, she would. No part of Aster was in a hurry to join the ranks of London matrons.

So much time was a gift, Prim realized. Once she was out in Society, there would be no foiling Mama's plans. She would be a veritable ringmaster, cracking the whip and marshaling Prim through her paces.

She should seize this time—embrace it.

The notion of staying in, all alone (on her birthday, no less!) made her feel like a tragic heroine. Well, not alone, she supposed. She would have Gertie for company. Her dour-faced former governess was not exactly the most cheerful of conversationalists. Presumably, that was something she had never been taught in governess training. Prim had shared many a silent dinner with her—except for Gertie slurping her soup and chewing her meat. She was a very loud eater.

Suddenly, Prim felt all the more tragic in the face of the lackluster evening looming before her.

Mrs. Zaher excused herself and it was just the two of them in the comfortable drawing room.

Olympia was prattling on about the recent salon she had attended with several of her mother's friends from the theater when Prim took a breath and interrupted her. "Your mother is correct. This is a special day for me."

Olympia nodded in agreement. "Of course, it is. You should have something more than tea and cakes and Gunter's."

"I agree. As you said, it should be marked in a grand fashion."

"You don't need to convince me."

"You know . . . it's bewildering. I always wanted to be out in Society. I thought that meant freedom, but now I think it will be the opposite."

"With your mother as chaperone? That is a certainty."

"I should count this time without Mama's attention on me as a gift."

"Yes! It is. You should live whilst you can!"

"Indeed, I should." Prim should not squander this time. Nodding slowly, she stroked her lower lip.

Olympia cocked her head and a small devilish smile played about her lips. She leaned forward with a conspiratorial air, her hands falling to her knees. "What are you planning in that brilliant mind of yours?"

"Me. You." Another breath. "Vauxhall. Tonight." The words came from some place deep inside her, as though they had been within her all along, lying in wait, ready and eager and yearning to spring free. "Can you imagine anything more exciting?"

Certainly, Vauxhall was a bold destination. A place she had fantasized about visiting one day. The outdoor pleasure gardens were a public venue where all manner of people congregated for entertainment, food, drink, and more. The kind of things that existed nowhere else. Music, art, fantastical illumination, awe-inspiring architecture. It was magical, the pride of London. Royalty visited there right alongside the commoners.

There was risk involved certainly. The evenings were purportedly raucous, but if she wanted adventure, it was where one went. If she was to feel alive, to taste true freedom, it would be worth it.

"Vauxhall?" Olympia blinked. "Only the two of us? At night?"

It was Prim's turn to don a devilish smile. "What's amiss? Scared?"

Olympia looked properly offended. "Of course not."

"Wouldn't you like to see me dressed in a gown that would send my mother into fits?"

Olympia's lips twitched. "I *would* like to see that indeed."

"Me in an actual gown? Or Mama in fits?"

Olympia giggled. "Both." She sobered and nodded resolutely. "Let's do this. I'll take care of the gown for you. I have just the dress. Well, *Mama* has just the dress. Your dimensions are alike."

"Should I dare to even ask?"

"With your hair, the choices are as obvious as they are limited."

Prim grimaced. "Pink?" she supplied. "Or peach?"

"Oh shush. You can wear more colors than that. Don't let your mother influence you. Your hair is beautiful."

Beautifully garish, Mama would say.

"So what color is it then?"

"Peach," Olympia admitted rather sheepishly.

"I knew it!"

"Or rather . . . apricot."

Prim stifled her laugh at Olympia's cross look. "Well, thank you, my friend. I would appreciate the loan of the gown. I can arrange my own hair before I come over." She'd had plenty of practice in her many idle afternoons, after all. She could manage an adequate coiffure. "I'll leave once my family departs for the night." Excitement hummed through her as she thought of the night ahead and all the things they could do. Prim started checking off on her fingers. "I want to stay out until dawn." She winced. "Or at least close to dawn." She would have to return before the staff woke and started about their daily duties.

"Mama will be out late," Olympia continued. "She's performing and whenever I don't accompany her, she arrives home about the time the street sweepers are making their rounds."

Prim's mind raced with the delightful possibilities ahead. "I want to dance and drink champagne . . . I want to see acrobats and fireworks and flirt with a handsome man."

"Primrose Ainsworth, you wicked, *wicked* creature. I confess, seeing you do all those things will be thrilling." Olympia gave her shoulder a little shove. "Are you very sure about this though? Your mother would never allow it. *My* mother would never allow it."

It was Primrose's turn to smile. "Then we shall be very careful to make certain they never find out."

~~Only the shabbiest of persons ever ride in a hack-~~
~~ney coach, and certainly never a lady . . . unless~~
~~she, too, wishes to be deemed shabby.~~

> —*Lady Druthers's Guide to*
> *Perfect Deportment and Etiquette*

Consider always that the destination
matters a great deal more than the
mode of transport.

Chapter Three

Primrose spent the late afternoon readying herself for the night ahead.

She washed, scrubbing her skin until it gleamed pink, and then brushed her hair until it crackled. She did this without assistance. Her mother and sisters required the aid of Gertie and the other housemaid for their evening plans, after all. Luckily, Prim was accustomed to doing a great many things on her own, so that was no hardship, and it may have raised suspicions if she suddenly needed help getting ready for what her family assumed to be a night at home.

Her mother's exclamations could be heard distantly throughout the house as she oversaw preparations for the evening. Poor Aster was receiving the brunt of her attentions. Mama never once checked in on Prim after they'd returned from their shopping trip. That allowed Prim a certain amount of liberty.

She carefully selected her reticule for the evening to match the gown she had yet to see. The beaded cream muslin should do well enough. She fished out her pin money from where she hid it in the back of her armoire and secured it in the bag. Tonight would not be free, but the dent in her funds would be worth it.

She took great pains with her hair, heating an iron in the grate and using it to form loose curls that she then pinned up as artfully as she could. She had watched Gertie and their other maid perform the task often enough on her sisters. She might be accustomed to doing for herself, but she did not possess their level of skill, so she definitely needed the additional time. The end result was satisfactory, if not impressive.

As the hour approached when her family would leave, she held her breath, hoping that they would not decide to seek her out and say good night.

Her birthday wish was granted. They did not stick their heads in her chamber. Mama could be heard shrieking in the distance that they were running late, and then the house fell blessedly silent.

That left one more hurdle: Gertie was expecting to take dinner with her.

Prim hastened to the dressing table and gingerly arranged a nightcap over her head. She had to conceal her hair. Gertie would wonder why it was arranged with such care for a simple dinner. Closing the drapes, Prim turned to put out the lamp, then climbed into bed, pulling the covers up to her chin, waiting with nervous breath.

The knock soon came. Gertie eased open the door and peeked her head into the chamber. "Primrose? Are you napping?"

45

Prim mumbled something incoherent, imagining it to be the sound someone might make when being roused from sleep.

Gertie advanced into the darkened room.

"Yes, just a bit. I'm not feeling well."

"Oh dear." Gertie sank down on the side of the bed. "What ails you?"

"My stomach . . . it's my womanly pains. Nothing serious."

"Oh, shall I fetch one of my willow bark tonics? They do wonders."

"No. I just prefer to rest."

"What of dinner? Would you like me to bring you something? Perhaps a soup?"

"I'm not hungry. I think I just need to sleep. I am certain I will wake refreshed if I just get some rest." She held her breath, hoping Gertie would accept her explanation and leave her for the night.

"Very well." Gertie patted her arm and lifted up from the bed. "I'll see you in the morning."

Prim held her breath, waiting even after Gertie departed the room for the sound of her footsteps fading down the corridor. And then another ten minutes or so just for good measure.

Then she was up, flying from the bed as though it were afire.

Prim manipulated the covers so that if someone peeked in, they would think she was asleep in bed. Her efforts, of course, wouldn't hold up to a close inspection, but she doubted anyone would look carefully.

She crept from her bedchamber and moved furtively through the house, taking the servants' stairs out to the back garden, hoping she did not bump into a member of the staff. Fortunately, she encountered no one. She eased the door shut behind her, making certain not to slam it and attract undue attention.

It was rather dispiriting, she realized, to be able to sneak out with such ease. It was almost as though no one cared about her—as though she could disappear entirely and her family wouldn't even notice.

Shaking off the glum thought, she rounded the house through the side gate, wiping sweating palms down her skirts. As they had planned earlier, Prim wore only a simple frock since she would be changing at Olympia's house into a different gown.

With the closing of the gate, Prim determined tonight would be wonderful. No more gloomy thoughts. It was her birthday. Who needed a *ton* party to have fun? She and her friend would make their own party.

It was still light out, and Prim hoped she didn't appear conspicuous darting across the street to Olympia's house.

Like this morning, the housekeeper was quick to answer.

"Come in, Miss Primrose. Olympia is in her bedchamber. She said for you to join her there. Shall I take your cloak and show you to—"

"No, thank you! I know the way, of course." With a wave and smile, she dashed up the stairs, careful to avoid the maid descending with an armful of linens.

She knocked once on Olympia's bedchamber door and then charged inside. She couldn't help herself. She was much too eager for this evening.

Olympia was already attired in her gown, and Prim gasped, her hand flying to her throat. "You look beautiful."

Olympia clasped a handful of skirts and twirled in a circle. "Thank you. I've been saving this for a special occasion . . . now let's get you out of that and into something more appropriate for an evening at Vauxhall." Her friend stood behind her and made short work of the tiny buttons at the back of Prim's dress.

In quick order, Prim was divested of garments and stripped down to her chemise. Even her corset was removed in exchange for one of Olympia's. "This here is a proper one that lifts you up as a corset should."

"Umph," Prim exclaimed as Olympia gave the laces a nearly violent tug. "Not so tightly, please. I'd care to eat tonight." *And breathe.*

"This is precisely how tightly Diana laces me in. Do you want me to ring for her? She will not have so gentle a hand."

"Need I remind you that I am not at all as accustomed to fitted corsets as you are," she pointed out.

"Oh very well." She let up a bit on the laces. "Better?"

"Yes. Thank you." She inhaled and exhaled with much more ease.

"There." Olympia helped slip the gown over her head. "You are magnificent."

Primrose turned to stand before the cheval mirror, aghast at the reflection of herself. She was a stranger to her own eyes. Her hand floated to her neckline and exposed décolletage.

Up until this moment she had not even realized she was in possession of quite so impressive a bosom. Or a bosom at all. Her fingers thrummed over all her bared skin. There was so very much of it.

She bit her lip for a long moment before releasing it to say, "I don't think I can wear this. It's . . . It's . . ." *Indecent.*

"Mind your tongue," Olympia admonished. "This is one of Mam's gowns you are wearing. I took it from her wardrobe."

"And I am certain she's perfectly lovely in it. It's acceptable for your mother to wear it. She's a woman full-grown. An entertainer, a performer. She is expected to dress in a manner more . . . adventurous."

Olympia made a sound that was part laugh and part snort. "Indeed. Mam is a most accomplished adventuress. This is true."

"Perhaps a fichu?" she suggested, moving to Olympia's dressing table and plucking up one of the frothy squares of fabric.

If a bodice even teased at a glimpse of cleavage, Mama insisted on tucking a fichu into the dress. Considering most of Prim's dresses were hand-me-downs from her older sisters and were not tailored specifically to fit, she always wore a fichu tucked down the front of her gown.

Primrose stroked a hand across the displayed flesh of her bosom again. In this daring neckline and wearing a corset the likes of which she had never worn before, she looked every inch a woman. Even older than her ten and six years. Mama would require her smelling salts were she to see Primrose now.

A smile played about her lips at the notion.

"Stop your fidgeting." Olympia gestured to herself. "Your gown is no more scandalous than mine and I promise we will be unexceptionally attired for Vauxhall. If we were to dress as we typically do?" She shook her head with a cluck of her tongue. "No, no, no. That, my dear, would create a spectacle. We would be much gawked upon in that event, and we want to fit in. *Not* stand out."

She had a valid point. Vauxhall was not for milksop misses or schoolgirls. It was for those of bold disposition and with a taste for adventure.

Vauxhall was for her tonight—or she vowed it would be.

"You are correct, of course." Prim smoothed a hand down her skirts, marveling at the quality of her gown, at the soft texture beneath her palm. The outer layer was an opaque India muslin. The apricot-colored underskirt beneath was silk sarsnet, imported from China. Neither was a fabric one would commonly find in the Ainsworth household. They were much too expensive. Papa would say such gowns were for those *without* an army of women beneath one roof.

Whenever Mama spied out the front parlor window at the Zahers arriving home with packages and parcels from all the best shops in Town, she would squawk loudly and turn on Papa.

"Mr. Ainsworth!" she would begin. "How is it that woman and her daughter can have such fine and beautiful things whilst we must economize?" She always spat out the word *economize* as though it were the foulest of epithets. Truly, it was foreign to her vocabulary. Papa had introduced her to it years ago.

Then Papa would look up from whatever he was doing and dryly reply, "Simple, dear. Mrs. Zaher has more money than we do."

Mama would puff up, her face reddening in outrage. "Well! If you're going to be so vulgar as to discuss money, I will leave you to your leisure."

"Prim." Olympia said her name with such seriousness that

Prim snapped out of her reverie and looked up from the scandal of her borrowed gown.

"Are you certain you are up for this? You don't have to do this. No one is forcing you. We could stay in and eat sweets and play whist—"

"No. I want to do this. I am ready." She squared her shoulders, ignoring the flow of cool air over her exposed chest, reaching for her earlier excitement. She ran a hand over her silky skirts. "This will be the only birthday celebration I have. Let us make it count. It will be a most memorable night. As long as you are willing, of course. I don't want you to be uncomfortable."

"The evening is not about comfort. It's about adventure, and I am more than willing." Smiling again, Olympia reached for their gloves on the nearby dressing table, handing Primrose hers. "It shall be brilliant."

Prim nodded, eager butterflies eddying through her. They each slid on their gloves and gathered up their reticules.

"Oh! And we mustn't forget these." Olympia brandished a pair of elegant masks. The goal was for no one to recognize them tonight. Not many people would be able to identify Primrose, as she lived a hermit's life, mostly confined to her home, but Olympia ventured out into Society a great deal. Unlike most debutantes, Olympia navigated Society for the sheer pleasure of it, without an agenda. Mrs. Zaher never pressured her daughter to acquire a husband, and Prim never heard Olympia mention that any gentlemen caught her eye. It must be nice to live without that manner of pressure.

In any event, Olympia would be easy to identify. The mask was important for her. Not so very important for Primrose, but she went along with it anyway. It added a dash of glamour and mysteriousness to the night ahead. Masquerades always seemed so romantic. Prim could be *anyone* she wanted.

"Very well." Prim took her domino from Olympia and slid it inside her reticule alongside her pin money. Once they were on their way, she would don the mask. She patted her reticule. "Let our adventure begin."

Mrs. Zaher was out for the evening, giving Olympia more freedom to come and go. The Zaher staff were accustomed to Olympia hopping back and forth across the street—and Prim dashing in and out. They didn't blink at their comings and goings. It was simple enough to slip away.

The housekeeper easily accepted the story that they were going to a dinner party with Prim's family, even going so far as to wave them farewell before closing the front door after them.

They strolled outside, at first walking in the direction of the Ainsworth house on the unlikelihood that anyone was watching them from the Zaher household. Hopefully no one in the Ainsworth household was peering out the window. Then they took a sudden turn and rounded the corner away from both their houses.

Prim looked around nervously.

"Look straight ahead. It's all about behaving as though you know where you are going and you have every right to go there," Olympia said beside her with an air of expertise.

"How are we getting there?" She had not even thought to inquire how they would arrive at the docks before taking a boat to Vauxhall. Only now did Primrose wonder at that first step of the night's escapade.

"As soon as we turn this next corner, we shall hail a hackney."

"A hackney?"

"What did you expect? Our coachman would not dare take us to Vauxhall, at least not without alerting Mam."

Prim simply had not thought much beyond sneaking out of her house and the fact that they needed to be back well before the first servants roused the following morning. She could not forget that. They would have to keep track of the time.

Excitement trembled through her. She was going to be out all night. For all her antics and peccadillos, she had never done anything like this before.

"Oh look! There's one!" Olympia took one step out into the street and waved over an approaching hackney with her usual easy confidence. The driver slowed and pulled to the side.

Her friend strode up to the door and pulled it open. She waved for Prim to precede her into the coach.

Primrose moved forward and then hesitated at the door. She glanced uncertainly at Olympia and inquired with a stab of misgiving, "Are you certain?"

"Don't lose your courage now," Olympia cheered.

Prim's chin shot up. She was in no way dissuaded from this evening's adventure. It was her idea, after all. Only she had not thought through the matter of transportation to their destination when she had declared this night's plan.

Mama always insisted that public conveyances were *common* and for ordinary folk, which the Ainsworths basically were, but Prim knew better than to point that out. It would only spark Mama's temper.

The coachman called down impatiently. "Are ye coming or not? I'm not making a fare sitting here waiting on ye lasses."

Primrose blinked. Never had anyone outside of her family spoken to her in such a direct manner.

Tonight, she imagined, would be a night of many firsts.

"We're ready," Prim answered. With a decisive nod, she ascended into the coach and settled onto the well-worn squabs. Olympia followed, calling up directions to the coachman as she did.

They fell back as the coach lurched forward, their hands falling onto the seat for steadying support.

"Ack!" Olympia exclaimed, lifting her hand from the velvet squabs. "There's something sticky on the fabric."

Primrose shuddered and carefully settled her hands into her lap so that they would no longer make contact with the cushion.

Olympia continued, "I don't even want to imagine what it could be."

Primrose nodded. "I wouldn't."

Olympia fished out a handkerchief from her reticule dangling from her wrist. She wiped clean her palm.

Olympia sighed with a nod. "Well, we are on our way now. Perhaps the hack we take on the return home will be nicer."

Prim would worry about that later. There was a score of other things to consider before then. Such as reaching Vauxhall. They still had yet to do that. *One obstacle at a time.*

As the coach continued its journey, they both reached for

their dominos. Prim helped Olympia when the ribbons of her mask became tangled in her lush dark curls, admiring them as she did so. What she wouldn't give for Olympia's raven locks. Her canary-yellow gown complemented her dark hair and skin perfectly.

Olympia followed suit, securing Prim's domino in place by tying the ribbons at the back of her head. It was a strange and liberating sensation to have her hair swept up off her neck.

When they arrived at the waterfront, several groups were already waiting for boats to take them down the Thames to the South Bank. Some groups were large. Some were not groups at all, but rather pairs, like Olympia and Primrose. All the ladies present were accompanied by gentlemen.

That gave Prim pause.

"Um. Olympia?" she murmured as scrutiny fell on them. *Them.* Two lone females.

Clearly there was an element of danger to their adventure that she had not considered until this moment. Well, in a fashion. She'd always recognized there was risk. That was why she had decided to sneak out to Vauxhall, of all places. She wanted something that made her heart race to happen, and Vauxhall was the sort of place where things happened.

She wanted something to look back on when Mama was dragging her from one event to the next, forcing her to dance with gentlemen she deemed suitable.

Gentlemen with bad breath and furry teeth and long nose hairs who happened to be decades older than Prim. In short, gentlemen not of the man-boy variety.

"You there! You two!" A woman in a garish red gown waved

them over. She and two other ladies were climbing into an awaiting boat. A single gentleman accompanied them.

The boatman followed the lady's gaze, spotting Olympia and Primrose. "We have room for two more! Come on with ye!"

Locking arms, Olympia and Primrose hastened forward over the dock.

Primrose dug a coin from her reticule and passed it into the hand of the waiting boatman, who then assisted them down into the vessel.

Clinging to each other for support within the less-than-steady conveyance, they sank down on one of the rows' plank seats.

"Thank you," Prim murmured to the lady in red and her companions as the boatman pushed off from the bank.

"Not at all, not at all, my dear," the lady chirped. "You looked a little lost up there on the dock and we had room for two more."

Prim and Olympia exchanged looks.

"This is our first visit to Vauxhall," Prim admitted.

"Oh la!" The lady in red slapped Primrose lightly with her fan. "You are in for a treat!"

The lone gentleman in their midst spoke up. "How old are you gels?"

"Reggie! For shame! You never inquire a lady's age," one of the other women in the boat admonished.

Reggie shrugged. "They barely look out of the schoolroom." He moistened his fleshy lips. "A fine pair of morsels they will make for some pair of libertines this eve."

Primrose felt her eyes widen behind her domino.

Olympia patted her hand reassuringly as she replied, "Indeed. Libertines far more polite than *you*, I am sure."

The other ladies laughed at her quick rebuttal.

Reggie scowled.

Obviously, Olympia was accustomed to the flirtations of lecherous gentlemen. Of course, she received numerous advances. She must. Not that she ever mentioned anything of the sort to Primrose, but she was lovely and would obviously come with a considerable dowry.

"Well done," Prim murmured.

Olympia shrugged. "As the daughter of an illustrious opera singer who hosts parties touting an assortment of colorful personages, I'm not entirely naïve in the ways of the world."

"Oh stop trying to scare them, Reg. Clearly, it does not work," the lady in red chided, and then turned back to Prim and Olympia. "Stay together. You will be fine, but don't go off on a darkened walk with anyone, lest you know what you are about." She dipped her chin and widened her eyes meaningfully.

Primrose nodded in understanding.

She might not be the most experienced in the ways of Society, but she was not naïve in the ways of the world. As the youngest of four sisters, and largely ignored by her family, she had overheard all manner of conversations not meant for her tender ears. Even their few servants tended to speak freely around her, as though she were simply part of the wallpaper. She was an expert observer.

Water lapped at the sides of the boat in a rhythmic cadence. The boatman worked steadily, the oars dropping and pulling through the water on either side of them its own lulling song.

Other boats dotted the dark waters of the Thames, some bigger, some actual ships with men crawling the riggings as deftly as monkeys and preparing for their imminent docking. She had never actually been on the river before. Her glimpses of it had been only from afar as she traveled in a conveyance, squashed on a seat between her sisters.

The boat rocked suddenly from a rogue wave and Prim clutched one side of the coasting vessel for support. Water sprayed her gloved fingers but she did not bring them back inside. She kept them where they were until the tips of her gloves were quite damp, exhilarated by this new sensation.

The group sharing the boat with them laughed and talked, but Prim could only stare around her as they glided south. She didn't digest a single word of their conversation. Instead she tipped her head to look up at the pink and gold streaked sky. Dusk was upon them.

The fading light of sunset cast the water's surface in fire. Incredibly, even with the not-so-aromatic smells of the river and the rotting refuse emanating from the nearby docks, it was magical.

Freedom was magical.

The bustling South Bank loomed ahead. There was a boat in front of them, and they had to linger in the water, rocking in place until it was their turn to row forward.

The boatman tied off the vessel on the dock and then helped them disembark.

"Have a care this eve'n, ladies," the woman in red trilled as she was swept away by her friends toward the lights and stirring sounds of Vauxhall Gardens just up the rise.

Primrose slipped off her gloves and stuffed them into her reticule. They were damp and the evening was warm. Besides, she didn't need any barrier between her and the world she was entering. She wanted to experience it all—right down to her fingertips.

They cleared the giant stone archway and paused. Vauxhall spread forth before them in all its magical, glittering splendor.

~~Once a lady's name appears in the scandal sheets~~
~~she might as well take her leave and eschew all~~
~~good Society.~~

> —*Lady Druthers's Guide to*
> *Perfect Deportment and Etiquette*

Perhaps fun is worth a scandal.

Chapter Four

"We're here. We are really here," Primrose said in wonder, looping her arm with Olympia's as they left the elaborate stone archway behind.

It was a feast for the eyes and Primrose did not know where to look—much less where to start. The air was alive, crackling with energy, the way it felt after a storm. She did not need to look down to know the tiny hairs on her arms were alive and vibrating.

As they advanced on the main row, the descending dark was obliterated in a burst of artificial light. *Aahs* and *oohs* filled the air in wonder at the impressive display of illumination.

A large row, wide enough for several carriages, loomed ahead. Tall sycamores and various structures marked the edges of the path. No carriages traveled the thoroughfare. People milled freely about and walked its length. Swarms of people. Women

in gowns of every shade, flaunting décolletage that made Primrose appear modest in her own dress, strolled the garden's
lantern-lit row, moving in seeming rhythm with the lively orchestra playing nearby in the bandstand. Even the gentlemen
were attired in vibrant colors and moved with harmony.

"There are so many people here," Prim marveled. She had
never seen such a multitude of people in one place at the same
time. Not at the park. Not out shopping. Indeed, it felt as though
half of London must be here. It was a festival of delights.

"Your eyes are glowing, Prim." Olympia chuckled with a
shake of her head and a happy squeeze of her fingers on Primrose's arm. "It is good to see you like this."

Like this. She meant *alive*. For years she had felt as though
she were in a dormant slumber. All her life, really. In a state
of perpetual waiting. Waiting for her life to begin, waiting to
make her debut, waiting to get married. The latter two both
things she no longer could even claim to want.

But this, she wanted. *Tonight.*

Olympia continued, "I fear we have created a monster and
you will want to do this every night."

Prim sobered a bit, some of her excitement deflating at the
thought of tomorrow. Tomorrow, when reality returned. For it
must return.

This would *not* be every night.

She knew better than to hope for more.

There would be no *more*.

Her earliest lessons, however much she had struggled against
them, had included the vital teaching of a woman's place in
polite society. Lady Druthers had seen to that. The guide that

she could recite from memory to this day had been all about conveying this lesson and more. A lady must protect her good name at all costs.

If Prim fell from grace, if her reputation was lost, then her family would suffer, too. Indeed, she would become unmarriageable, but Aster would pay the price, as well. As Prim's one sister who had not yet secured a betrothed, she likely never would if scandal befell the family. Correction: if Primrose brought scandal upon their house.

Ruin was contagious. It contaminated everyone in a family.

Primrose might struggle to get along with her parents and sisters, but she did not wish them ill. Especially not Aster. She'd felt Aster's pain as she had navigated her *second* season, and she continued to empathize, feeling Aster's despair as she endured her third. All the debutantes who debuted with Aster were either engaged or married now. Some were already expecting their first child. Aster needed to land a match, if only to satisfy their mother, and Primrose would not engage in risky behavior beyond this night and endanger Aster's chance for that.

Just this once, Prim would do it for herself. And never again.

"No. Not every night," she told her friend firmly. "Only tonight."

So Prim would make it count. She'd make every moment of this evening matter.

"What shall we do first?" Olympia asked. She gestured vaguely. "Should we get something to drink? And eat?"

"Yes." Although the volley of butterflies in her stomach might not have agreed. "That sounds brilliant." She searched their surroundings and then pointed down the main row. "A tavern?"

Prim squinted at the name over the door. "The Rose and the Dove? That sounds promising. Very Shakespearean."

"What about one of the pavilions?" Olympia asked. "Perhaps we could find a vacant supper box?"

Primrose considered that, glancing from a curtained pavilion to the tavern. A *tavern*. When would she ever have the chance to visit a tavern again? Proper young ladies did not frequent such places. And maybe, after she was married, she'd be invited to a supper box, where the *ton* often rubbed elbows. But never a tavern.

She looked back to Olympia and smiled her most cajoling grin.

Olympia chuckled. "You want to go in the tavern, don't you?"

She nodded. "Yes! Just to see what it's about."

Olympia nodded. "Well, tonight is about firsts and that would be a first even for me. Let us go then."

They continued down the row to The Rose and the Dove, standing to the side as a rowdy group of patrons tumbled out through the front door. One of the gentlemen lost his balance and fell into them. He gripped Prim's shoulder amid a laughing fit in an attempt to steady himself.

"Unhand her!" Olympia swung her reticule at him.

"Ouch!" He flinched, rubbing at his cheek.

No longer laughing, he focused on Primrose, his bleary-eyed gaze roaming her face and head. "My apologies, Red."

Red?

She squared her shoulders in affront at his familiarity . . . but there was a small dose of exhilaration mixed in there too.

This was truly happening. She was here at Vauxhall Gardens rubbing elbows with the general public.

"I prefer . . . Scarlet," Prim loftily intoned. Anyone could be someone. Or no one. There were no formalities. No introductions required.

It was liberating.

The man eyed them warily as he stumbled off with his friends.

Olympia sent her a wink. "Welcome to Vauxhall, eh? Mam did describe it as rowdy. At least that's why she makes excuses not to bring me here."

They passed through the entryway and scanned around them at the carousing patrons. Primrose was confident she was observing the effects of over-imbibing. It seemed to be in evidence everywhere. On rare occasions, Papa indulged in his port and waxed on about his youth, his eyes shining like glass as he reminisced. She suspected she would observe a goodly amount of glassy-eyed individuals tonight.

The door thudded shut behind them, muffling the orchestra and all other outside sounds, leaving them with the undiluted experience of the tavern.

The establishment was crowded. A woman with an improbable shade of red hair and wearing a garish orange gown — not the best color on anyone, and Prim would know — stood on a small stage along one wall singing to the accompaniment of flutists. The entertainment, while not as skillful as Mrs. Zaher's performances, was no less entertaining.

"See there." Olympia nodded to the stage as they wove

through the room, locating a vacant table. "You bemoan your hair while there are those desperate to replicate it."

Sinking down at the table, Olympia waved over a nearby server with all the expertise and authority of a veteran patron. It took a while for the aproned lass to wind through the crowd of tables to reach them.

"What can I fetch you, ladies?" she asked breathlessly.

"How is the mulled wine?" Olympia asked, as though it were a common practice for her to order spirits at taverns.

The lass looked left and right and then leaned forward to answer. "Were I you, I'd have the ratafia."

"Two ratafias it is." Primrose nodded emphatically.

The server grinned. "Fine choice. I will be back soon with your drinks, ladies."

Once she was gone, Primrose inspected their surroundings further. Several people were joining in, warbling along with the singer's bawdy song. Apparently it was a well-known ditty.

A Lusty young Smith at his Vice stood a Filing,
Rub, rub, rub, rub, rub, rub in and out, in and
    out ho.

Olympia laughed. "Mam should sing this at Haymarket."

"You will have to share the lyrics with her."

Olympia's eyes widened at the suggestion. "Mam might be more tolerant than your mother, but even *she* would suffer apoplexy were she to know where I am sitting right now."

Primrose considered her for a moment, feeling a sharp prick

at her conscience. She had scarcely given thought to Olympia or how any whiff of scandal might affect her and her mother.

Her friend always seemed to have so many more freedoms than Prim, but of course even Mrs. Zaher would not approve of this night's exploits. An unchaperoned trip to Vauxhall? Indeed not. And yet Prim had insisted on this adventure for herself, bringing Olympia out with her.

"I appreciate you taking such risks to go against your mother for me. I would never want you to get in trouble. I know how close the two of you—"

Olympia waved her hand. "Hush, now. You've been my dearest friend since Mam and I moved here three years ago. What is youth without a little bit of rebellion? I am certain my mother expects it of me."

Prim laughed. "That's one way to look at it."

Olympia continued, "And you well know not every girl in this city has been kind and welcoming to me. They talk about me in indiscreet tones, as though I cannot hear their petty remarks about my looks. Mam they welcome because she is wealthy and a celebrity." Mrs. Zaher had toured all over the continent, performing for even royalty. "Me they simply tolerate." She wrinkled her nose. "Just barely."

Prim's mother called Mrs. Zaher and Olympia scandalous. *It's shameful the way that woman takes her daughter everywhere with her as though it was appropriate. A girl of such tender years does not belong at the opera. It's unseemly!*

Papa took a different stance. He insisted that Mrs. Zaher was merely an eccentric artist and allowances could be made as she was so admired among the *ton*. *Leave it be, Mrs. Ainsworth. Socialization betwixt the girls can only benefit our Primrose.*

For no other reason did Mama allow the association between them. It was because of Papa's logic alone. If their friendship was perceived as a benefit to Primrose, then it would be perceived as a benefit to the entire family.

If others voiced their disapproval of Mrs. Zaher taking her young daughter all about Town, it did not influence her—quite the opposite. Prim had heard both Mrs. Zaher and Olympia comment, although never with any heat or acrimony, that the British were far too conventional.

Mrs. Zaher lived her life as she wished, giving no tribute to English customs. Perhaps Mrs. Zaher followed the customs of Andalusia, where she and Olympia had originally lived? Likely not though. Prim suspected Mrs. Zaher followed her own rules and lived by a code of her own creation.

Prim breathed in deeply, marveling as she did so. Could there be any greater freedom than the power to flout social conventions? She felt a thrill in knowing she was doing that very thing now.

Sometimes, late at night, she'd hear carriage wheels clattering down the sleeping streets of Belgrave Square, and she would dash to her window to watch as Mrs. Zaher and Olympia descended from their carriage, glittering and sparkling in their finery. Envy burned hot in her chest on those evenings, eating its way up her throat. She had always longed to do the things Olympia did, to be similarly close with her own mother . . . but Prim knew that even once Mama allowed her out into the world, it would never be like that. She would never have a special relationship with her mother . . . and Mama would never grant her independence.

Prim shook her head, chasing away such maudlin thoughts. Now was not the time to think about things she could not change.

Now was the time to enjoy herself.

Their drinks arrived. In unison they lifted their cups in a toast.

"To friendship," Prim intoned, "I wouldn't want to do this with anyone else."

"Aw." Olympia pressed a hand over her heart. "And to birthdays," she added. "May they all be as memorable as this one."

They clinked cups and took their first sip.

Primrose gave a satisfying sigh and lowered her cup to the table. The serving girl was right. The ratafia was excellent. Her first taste of spirits was all she'd hoped it would be.

"Certain, are you, that this birthday will be so very memorable?" Prim asked playfully.

"Is it not already?"

Primrose considered that. Even if they left following this drink, she would have done more than she ever had before—and more than she would likely do once Aster was engaged and Mama turned her full attention to Prim. It would be no easy matter to sneak away then. Not even to the bookshop while Mama napped.

"Simply seeing Vauxhall has made for a most memorable evening. Sitting in a tavern? Drinking spirits?" She lifted her cup. "These are all things I've never done." The evening was off to a good start. She took another drink.

69

"Shall we eat here then?" Olympia asked. "Or explore some of the vendors along the row?"

Prim had not given much consideration to their dining plans, although her stomach grumbled in protest. At home, she would have eaten by now.

Mostly, she had considered all the many things she should like to *see* at Vauxhall. She had read so much about the pleasure gardens. It was the spectacle of all spectacles. She knew one evening would not allow for every attraction. Prim needed to consider what she wanted to see and do the most before the night ended.

"Oh! We should make our way to one of the acrobatic demonstrations. I understand there are contortionists and tightrope walkers, too." Taking another sip of ratafia, Prim scanned the tavern again, marveling at the array of people—all ages and sizes. Prim had never seen such a variety of dresses. At one corner table, a lady wore a bright purple jacket and matching striped trousers. Her legs were crossed elegantly as she conversed with her companions and smoked a pipe.

"Oh, and we must not miss the fireworks," Olympia chimed in.

Prim could not stop studying her surroundings. It was a banquet for the eyes.

At a nearby table, another lady wore a turban with peacock feathers dancing high in the air at least twenty inches above her head. A young man beside her continually swatted at one of the drooping feathers, earning glares and sharp words from her. The rest of their table mates, like so many of the tavern's patrons, hooted at the singer, calling out song requests.

As entertaining as it was, Prim was ready to venture outside.

She knew the Gardens to be vast. There was much to do and the night was waning. "Let's finish these drinks and then return to the row and see what else is afoot," she suggested.

Olympia nodded and resumed drinking.

Primrose returned her attention to the stage and the impressive flutists who far outshone the singer.

Suddenly a shriek carried over the performers and the general din of the tavern. Prim jerked, startled, and searched for the source, glimpsing a man going down in a sudden blur, knocked from his chair to the floor by another man.

The lady who had been sharing the table with him jumped from her seat and launched herself at the offender with no thought to decorum or personal safety. She was a virago, a veritable Boudicca.

Prim could only gawk at the woman as she locked one arm around the howling man's neck in a stranglehold and pulled him by the hair with her other hand. His body twisted and flailed in a frenzied attempt to escape, spinning them both into a nearby table and sending those occupants crashing from their seats to the floor.

It was a cascade effect at that point.

More people fell into each other, colliding and then pushing one another.

Tables overturned.

Pottery and dishware shattered.

Women screamed. Men hollered. Fists swung.

It was an utter melee. And amid the riot of people, she spotted a familiar face. Her stomach twisted.

A wretchedly familiar face.

"Olympia!" She seized her friend's hand and tugged her down, taking them both under the shelter of their table.

Olympia shrank close to the pedestal base as a dish shattered near her slippered foot, spraying them with shards that, thankfully, did not penetrate through their voluminous skirts.

"I think we need to try for the door." Olympia started to stand, but Prim yanked her back down to the dirty floor.

"We can't go. *I* can't," she hissed. Now there was suddenly more to fear than getting maimed in a brawl.

"What are you talking about?"

"I can't be seen. Violet's betrothed. He's here. Redding is here!" Her hand flew to her domino, as though needing to assure herself it was still in place. "Perhaps he won't recognize me."

Olympia winced. "How many times has he been in your company?"

Prim bit her lip and contemplated the question.

She might not be included at many adult functions, but he was her sister's fiancé. There had been many occasions when they shared the same space. "Half a dozen. Perhaps more," she offered, "But he usually ignored my presence—"

"If he comes face-to-face with you, he will know you at once." Olympia pointed to her head. "That hair of yours is far too distinctive."

A woman screamed. Prim flinched and dug her fingers into the pedestal base of their table as though it could anchor her in the swelling chaos.

A body landed near their table. It was a man. A woman sat atop him, slapping him over and over with her reticule. It looked painful. The man grunted from each and every blow.

Still squatting, Prim shuffled around the table's base, crowding closer to Olympia, trying to get as far as she could from the violence erupting inches away from her.

Crack.

Their table suddenly splintered. The remnants shattered around them, leaving them exposed and vulnerable. They couldn't remain hunkered down on the floor, out in the open like this. It wasn't safe. They had to stand lest they be trampled.

People were stampeding. Bodies bumped into them with no consideration. Hands shoved. Elbows jabbed. Shoulders butted into her, spinning her around.

Prim struggled against the pandemonium, clinging to Olympia's hand, but suddenly they were ripped apart. Helpless to fight it, Prim was swept up in the current. Even as she was dragged along, she strained and searched for a glimpse of her soon-to-be brother-in-law. Best to know his location so as to avoid him.

Again, she spotted him.

He was laughing and having a jolly time as bodies tangled in battle around him. His companions punched and kicked, taking as many blows as they delivered. Redding snatched a bottle of wine from a nearby table that was miraculously not yet overturned.

Grinning like an idiot, he tucked himself under the table and took several deep swigs from the bottle of wine, observing the fray as though taking in a performance at Haymarket.

He really was a fool, and soon to be a member of her family.

Just then, the dolt turned his face in her direction and she squeaked, dropping low again, which resulted in her being knocked over amid trouncing feet.

She cried out and brought her knees up to her chest, ignoring the fair amount of ankle she was no doubt revealing. She covered her head, trying to protect herself from the bodies thrashing all around her.

Splendid.

She'd not been here even an hour and her night had devolved into this. It would all come to an end when she was crushed to death on a tavern room floor.

Someone's boot struck her in the shoulder blade. "Ouch!" She rubbed at the afflicted area.

This was far from the adventure she had envisioned.

"Olympia!" she cried out, hoping her friend was faring better.

Suddenly, she was swept up off the ground by arms far too strong and big and masculine to belong to her friend. Prim squawked, her legs thrashing.

"Easy there, Miss," a gruff voice assured her. "I'll get you out of here."

"I am quite capable of walking," she protested even as some of the panic ebbed out of her. She was no longer under direct threat of being crushed, at least.

She ceased to struggle as she scanned for Olympia.

Where was her friend?

Prim twisted her neck around, desperate to locate Olympia. Fortunately, her canary-yellow gown stood out in a crowd and Primrose spied her across the tavern. *Far* across the tavern.

Somehow they'd grown quite distant from each other—and seemed to be growing only farther and farther away as Prim was being carried. "Olympia!"

The length of the tavern stretched between them with tussling bodies in the way. Prim's rescuer was carrying her in the opposite direction of her friend, and that could not happen.

Primrose extended an arm as though that could do some good, as though she could reach her. "Olympia!" she shouted again.

Olympia heard her. Her head shot up and their gazes locked. Her friend was near the tavern's front door now.

Prim was being carried in the opposite direction. She opened her mouth to object, to insist that the stranger, well-meaning though he may be, put her down at once so that she could make her way back to Olympia's side.

Suddenly, Redding filled her line of vision. *Oh no!*

He was barreling toward her, so close that with a shift of his gaze, he would spot her.

Panicked, Prim ducked her masked face, burying her head in the stranger's shoulder, effectively hiding herself.

Her heart thundered in her ears as she was carried. Hope beat hard and swift inside her. Certainly — *hopefully* — Redding would not notice her hair amidst the chaos all around them. How often did men really notice such things anyways?

The gentleman who carried her smelled surprisingly nice. Clean. She took a deeper sniff of his shoulder. A blend of . . . sandalwood? And the fabric of his jacket was soft and of fine quality.

Realizing she was conspicuously inhaling the scent of the man who carried her in his arms, she pulled her nose slightly away — and was then assailed with different odors.

The air quality felt different—by no means fresher, but the smells were different—a mix of foods, cigar smoke, colognes, and, in the distance, the pungent musk of the River Thames.

A door slammed and suddenly she was deposited on her feet. She swayed for a moment until a firm hand steadied her.

Prim was outside, free of the rowdy tavern.

She lifted her face to the flow of air and blinked against the night, peering around her and trying to take measure of her surroundings, feeling exposed and vulnerable without Olympia at her side.

This was not the well-lit main row that she had trod upon entering the Gardens. It was not totally wanting of light, but close enough, with only one lamp marking the narrow alley that ran behind the tavern and its neighboring establishment. The stink of trash from a nearby repository laced the air, the rank odor stinging in her nose.

A few other people, also intent on escaping the tavern brawl, stumbled out the door after them. Prim collapsed against the side of the building to catch her breath, rubbing at her sore shoulder. The others quickly made their way from the alley, leaving the backstreet eerily devoid of people.

Prim pushed to her feet and shook out her skirts, facing her rescuer, words of gratitude on her lips dying a swift death as her eyes clapped on the man before her. She could summon forth only a single awe-stricken word. *"You."*

Chapter Five

Primrose instantly regretted her sharply flung *you*.

For one thing, it rang out almost accusingly in the air. What if the much-too-handsome gentleman did not recognize her? She was wearing a mask, after all. Whatever the case, she had just informed him that *she* knew *him*—that man-boy had indelibly stamped himself on her memory.

Splendid.

He inclined his head—his lush dark hair beckoning touch as much as a field of spring-fresh grass. She shook her head, dismissing the whimsical thought.

"And you are the young lady who was with the illustrious Mrs. Zaher earlier today at Gunter's?"

She swallowed. Well, Olympia was correct. The domino was little good at concealment if someone had seen her before.

"Um. Yes. It's the hair, I suppose?" she asked rather baldly,

~~A proper introduction is required before a gentle-~~
~~man may speak to a lady. If such civility is cir-~~
~~cumvented, rest assured the lady's reputation is~~
~~also forfeit.~~

—*Lady Druthers's Guide to*
Perfect Deportment and Etiquette

The rules of civility are more
suggestions than rules.

reaching up to touch her strands. "Is that how you recognized me?"

He clasped his hands behind his back and gave a slight nod. "It is rather distinctive. And I only just saw you this day."

"Yes. Just." She frowned, feeling a failure. *Blast.* So much for not being recognized. He did not know her name, but he knew Mrs. Zaher. It was an altogether uncomfortable situation and made the possibility of discovery on a larger scale feel much too likely.

For now, though, the only discovery Prim needed to worry about was finding her friend.

"I realize we have not been properly introduced . . ." His voice faded and he glanced toward the tavern door. "Are you here with Mrs. Zaher? Or your . . . chaperone perhaps?"

At the mention of a chaperone, she winced. "I—er, am here with a friend. A friend I must now locate. Immediately."

"Of course." The young man nodded very properly. "I, too, have become separated from my friends. I saw you were struggling. Forgive me for being so forward. I did not mean to offend. I wanted only to help."

"Oh? You don't normally fling ladies over your shoulder like a sack of grain?"

His mouth twitched. "No, it's not my typical behavior."

"That is good to know."

They stared at each other for a long, awkward moment before he gestured ahead with a clearing of his throat. "It does not seem anyone else is fleeing this way. Shall we round to the front and locate our parties?"

79

She could not fault that logic. "Yes," she murmured.

He held out his arm to her, and she hesitated before taking it, then reasoned that it would be strange if she did not—and she was all for making this encounter feel less awkward. He'd carried her out of the brawling tavern, after all. It would not be such a breach at this point if she accepted his arm for escort. At any rate, the sooner she took his arm, the sooner this interaction could come to an end.

They left the quiet backstreet and rejoined the population steadily swarming along the main row. She rested her fingers on his sleeve very softly, barely touching. That seemed only proper. Well, not touching him *at all* would be the most proper thing to do, but she was well past propriety the moment she snuck out from her house and entered Vauxhall. She was well *well* past propriety the moment she and he started speaking without proper introduction.

Those few words exchanged at Gunter's hardly constituted a break in propriety. The exchange had mostly been between him and Mrs. Zaher, and as Olympia's mother was a notable pubic figure, that was not so very irregular. Strangers spoke to her all the time, praising and complimenting her performances. No one lifted an eyebrow over the interactions. Well, aside from Prim's mother. Lifting her eyebrows at the Zahers was one of her most favored pastimes. Second only to lifting her eyebrows at Prim.

This—what was happening now between her and man-boy—would lift Mama's eyebrows so high they would disappear into her hairline. But then again, this was Vauxhall. Purportedly everything that occurred here tonight would qualify as a scandal and send Mama into the vapors.

As they stepped out from the back alley and strode beneath the lanterns dotting the main row, she battled an overwhelming sense of vulnerability. Prim felt as though her mask had been ripped away. He knew she was connected to the Zahers. He could easily discover her identity if he was so inclined.

They approached the front of the tavern and stopped, scanning their surroundings. Prim recognized several people from inside the tavern now lingering about, but no bright canary dress in sight.

"Do you see your friend?" he asked.

"No." Frowning, she shook her head.

He motioned down the row. "Shall we continue down the path a ways? See if they're searching for us ahead?"

She nodded jerkily and together they proceeded.

A few moments passed and then she gave herself a little shake, realizing she had not asked him in turn. "What of you? Do you see your friends?"

"No, unfortunately."

They fell into an uneasy silence—at least on her part.

She was so flustered. She fought the urge to lift her hand away from his arm, and instead took a deep breath. She needed to focus on finding Olympia.

"Have you been here before?" Her companion's deep voice broke through the silence between them, politely inquiring. She swallowed back the thick lump of anxiety in her throat and willed her heart to cease its gallop.

Young men did not speak to her. She did not speak to them. There had been no occasion for it as of yet. Aside from Begonia's husband and Violet's betrothed, she had not been in the company of gentlemen for any notable amount of time.

And truth be told, in the case of her brother-in-law and her soon-to-be brother-in-law, she opted not to speak to either one of them.

Begonia's Milton was a bore who scarcely spoke at all, and when he did it was usually on the matter of the grade of mutton on his plate or his hopes for a son. Her sister had graced him with only daughters thus far. Something for which he faulted her entirely. The wretched man was rather vocal in that grievance.

Violet's betrothed had never acknowledged Prim's presence, which was a clear enough message. Redding thought her beneath his notice—perhaps because she was homely, young, female, or all of the above. She could only hazard a guess.

The young man beside her was unquestionably Quality, possibly even peerage, which made him far superior in station to her and anyone in her family or acquaintance.

Redding and Milton would fall over themselves to have even a nod from a man like this, no matter his tender years. If he was, in fact, a peer, it made him coveted company to her social-climbing brothers-in-law—*and* Mama. And yet here was this man-boy speaking to her as if she were an equal, behaving as though he valued what she had to say. More courtesy than Milton or Redding had ever shown her. Heavens, her own mother scarcely had time to listen to her.

Then again, these were rather extenuating circumstances,

and the least he could do was make some polite conversation, considering his hand had gripped dangerously close to her derrière.

He was still waiting for her answer. As though it mattered. As though *she* mattered. It was such a novel experience, she could not yet fully grasp it.

"Do I seem like a veteran of Vauxhall?" It was actually thrilling if he thought that—if he saw her as that sophisticated and urbane. She preened a little, dipping and angling her chin in what she imagined was a coquettish pose.

"No. You seem young. Too young for this place."

Her chin shot back up with indignation. She bristled. She did not appreciate the observation. For obvious reasons. Her youth was a sore subject and the weapon Mama used against her.

"I cannot be much younger than you, my lord," she countered.

He flinched before inclining his head in mild agreement. "True enough. I only just turned ten and nine a fortnight ago."

"Not so much older than me then."

"And yet I feel ancient." He smiled as he said this, but she sensed he was not entirely jesting. There was a current of sincerity running beneath his words.

"At least you are not ten and six and treated more as though you *are* six."

"Is that why you've ventured out tonight? To feel as though you are not a child? I must say you put yourself at peril for such a trivial goal."

Trivial?

She stopped to face him, not liking his tone of condescen-

sion—as though he believed her a silly creature here for frivolity and nothing deeper. "You speak as though you know me. You do not, my lord."

His head whipped left and right, looking around them at the many strolling people about their pleasures. "Jacob," he quickly supplied, a touch of urgency in his voice.

"I beg your pardon?"

"My Christian name is Jacob. Please do not address me so formally. I am no 'lord' and I needn't have people think it."

He was not? Everything about him proclaimed him Quality.

He continued, "Simply call me Jacob."

He wished her to be familiar with him? She shook her head. Impossible. They should not even be speaking in this manner at all.

"No. I cannot use your Christian name—"

"I insist. I prefer anonymity whilst here."

She frowned and glanced around. People milled about. Several sent them curious looks from where they stood. For all she knew, someone had already overheard her address him.

He gestured to her domino. "I would think you could understand the wish for anonymity."

But call him Jacob? "It's not proper," she insisted.

Annoyance flashed across his face and she wondered if that was common for him. Was he that breed of blueblood?

Did any other kind exist?

Weren't they all haughty? Over-privileged and short-tempered with those they deemed beneath them?

For obvious reasons, Prim had never rubbed elbows with Quality before (or people, in general, for that matter). But she

read of their exploits in the scandal rags, and she heard her family speak of all their deeds—especially their misdeeds.

Even Olympia and her mother shared in the gossip. There was one particular lord so enamored of Mrs. Zaher, he sent her flowers after every performance and rarely missed a show. He'd proposed to Mrs. Zaher no fewer than four times. Of course, that was exactly how many times he had been married before, and each one of his past wives had expired under vague circumstances. Even more alarming, it was rumored that every single previous wife had died shortly after he made the acquaintance of his next wife, and he always remarried as soon as propriety would allow.

I've no wish to be wife number five. Can you imagine? Mrs. Zaher had shuddered as she shook her head. *Who knows how long it would take until I'd meet my demise?*

Vice, Prim had decided, unfairly or not, was more rampant among the blue-blooded sector of Society. Especially among the men. Women, even ladies, had to take care of their reputations lest they be cast out. The gentlemen had little accountability and could get away with dastardly deeds.

"*You* are so concerned with propriety?" He asked as though that came as a surprise.

Her temper pricked at his clear insinuation. Prim let go of his arm, disliking his tone. He was no longer the only one annoyed now. He did not think her concerned with propriety? Well, on this night, she was not. True enough. But while she may have temporarily cast aside the trappings of decorum, she did not appreciate his judgment of her.

He did not know anything about her. Excluding the facts

that it was her birthday and she was acquainted with Mrs. Zaher, and that her hair was a rather unfortunate shade of red.

But other than that, he knew absolutely nothing.

Prim sniffed as though scenting something foul. What a cad, showing his airs as if he weren't partaking in the pleasures of Vauxhall himself. She did not care for his attitude one whit— or rather, she did not care for him.

"Just because I am at Vauxhall does not mean I've lost all sense of correctness."

"I did not say that." No, but he'd said enough. He'd called her motivations trivial and criticized her decision to be here.

"How *correct* can *you* be? *I* would never be so unkind as to insult a lady . . . er, if I were a gentleman that is. Or even if I weren't a gentleman." She winced a little. She was babbling. "I would not insult a person at all."

She suffered a quick stab of guilt at the memory of all the times she had joined Aster in poking fun at Violet when she returned from Bond Street with some ridiculous confection that she insisted was the height of fashion. Prim shoved the memory aside. Violet was a sister. Insults were their love language.

"It was not my intention to insult you."

"And why are *you* here?" She pointed at him. "Why is it acceptable for you and not me?"

"I—I am . . . older . . . and . . ." he sputtered, and she knew he was on the verge of declaring himself a man in the belief that that gave him an advantage—as it almost always did in this world.

"A prig?" she queried, blinking innocently.

He narrowed his eyes. "No."

"I have every right to be here," she went on to insist.

"Do you?" He angled his head as though skeptical of that.

"I may not be officially out in Society, but —"

"Wait. What?"

"What?" she echoed, uncertain of what she had just said that made his eyes round with incredulity, but already regretting it.

"Let me be clear. Not only have you snuck out from your home, but you are not even formally out in Society?"

"Oh." Perhaps she should not have mentioned that. She took a bracing breath. "As diverting as this has been, I really do need to find my friend."

He expelled a rough laugh. "Diverting?" He glanced around as though needing a reminder of their surroundings to fuel his outrage. "You ventured out to Vauxhall and you have not even entered Society yet?" Clearly he was not ready to let go of that.

"I came here with my friend unescorted and in secret. We've donned dominos for discretion." She touched her mask as though to verify it was still in place.

He scoffed. "Let us not even feign that it offers any true concealment."

She stiffened at his tone. "I do not understand why this matters to —"

He shook his head as though he had not heard her. "It ought to matter to *you*. It's quite one thing for you to sneak out with a friend to Vauxhall for an evening, but you're not even yet out of the schoolroom and here you are in this iniquitous den —"

"I've finished my schooling," she hotly protested. "I'm scarcely a child." This felt eerily similar to arguing with her mother.

"What could you have been thinking? You've yet to learn to navigate a ballroom. What made you think a night at Vauxhall would be simple to manage?"

"Most girls my age are already out in Society."

"Except you are not."

"It is merely because my mother is too overwrought attending to my sisters. One is marrying in a fortnight and the other is in her third season. I'll get my turn." She was babbling and could not seem to stop. Words poured from her in a torrent. "Once the wedding is over and Aster has a suitor, it will be my turn to—"

"You should not be here." He nodded as though this was the only point that mattered.

Except his opinion did not matter.

She squared her shoulders. "Well, fortunately for me, you have no authority over my choices."

"As a gentleman, I must insist—"

"As a gentleman, you can stuff it."

He blinked, clearly astonished at her aggressive language. She could understand that. She was shocked at herself, too. She'd admired him earlier today, his good looks leaving her tongue-tied, and now she was snapping at him as though they were familiars. Granted, he had rescued her from the tavern brawl, but why did he affect her so? It was odd.

And yet that realization did not stop her. What was he waiting for? A medal from the king for rescuing damsels? She was certainly *no* damsel.

She pressed on: "Force your will elsewhere. I'm sure there are servants waiting to do your bidding. I, fortunately, don't have to." She motioned to the tavern. "I really need to return inside and look for my friend."

He crossed his arms over his chest. "Unaccompanied?"

There was that judgment again. "Do you have a better suggestion?" She lifted her chin.

Her mother had demonstrated imperious behavior over the years. Primrose knew how it was done. Not only did she recognize it in others, she could imitate it. In fact, she could most expertly convey haughty disdain. She had practiced it behind Mama's back often enough to the amusement of Aster and even Violet. Her sisters were always devotees of her imitations.

The Ainsworths might not have been nobility, but Mama did not let that stop her from acting like it. She had hoped that one day they would legitimately be peerage, after all. Much to Mama's disappointment, her two eldest had failed in that endeavor, decisively putting an end to her dream.

Mama considered Aster and Primrose her least eligible daughters and had no ambitions for them to marry into the peerage. Truthfully, Primrose had to agree with her mother on that score. Aster was cripplingly shy, especially around gentlemen, and the list of Primrose's faults was long and extensive. Her wanton hair, her indecorous spots—her penchant for talking without forethought—to name just a few of her mother's complaints. *At least only one of my daughters has such wretched hair and spots on her face,* Mama would state from time to time

Prim didn't know from whom she may have inherited her smart mouth, but there had been a great Aunt Josephine, a spinster, on Papa's side. She died before Prim was born, but apparently she had possessed fiery-red hair and freckles. It almost felt like an omen. Aunt Josephine had never married, and spent her entire life caring for her elderly parents until they passed of natural causes due to old age. *Very* old age.

Prim suspected that if her fate were the same, she would be the one to go to the grave first.

Prim started for the tavern.

Man-boy fell in beside her. "I don't think you know at all what you are about here," he insisted in that deep voice of his.

She stopped and glared at him.

He continued, "Vauxhall is not suitable for unchaperoned ladies." Suddenly his voice did not sound so appealing to her ears.

"I do not require a chaperone at the moment. I am quite capable." Truth be told, she was beginning to tire of this conversation. It wasn't as though she was going to go steal away to one of the dark walks. Even if she had not already been warned, she knew better than that.

The dark walks of Vauxhall were a vast labyrinthine network of paths famous for all manner of vice — assignations being the foremost.

"That remains to be seen . . . and I did just happen to rescue you from being trampled on a tavern floor. You did not strike me as entirely capable when I was carrying you from the tavern."

"It is very boorish of you to fling that back at me, *my lord*."

Yes, it was petty of her to address him as though he possessed a title, and so very loudly, *and* after he had asked her not to, but she could not help herself. He was a wretch.

He glanced around a touch desperately. "Would you kindly

cease with the formal address? I don't need everyone thinking me—"

"A complete nob?" Yes. She relished saying that overly loud.

His nostrils flared. "You are quite the most vexing individual."

She was vexing?

He was the one being so arrogant, volunteering his very *unsolicited* opinions regarding her behavior.

Handsome men, she suddenly decided, were overrated.

She was quite done with this—and him. She had not slipped free from her yoke to have this stranger order her about. She needed to find Olympia. Perhaps they would laugh about this in the morning, but presently it felt imperative to find her friend.

Prim waved a hand at him dismissively in farewell. "You've been helpful. Thank you. But I am perfectly fine and not your responsibility."

Her annoyance with him was disproportionate, perhaps, but this night was to be *her* night, and it had already gone wildly off track. It was time to find her friend and get back to her adventure—an adventure that did not include arrogant young men.

~~A lady should never find herself in a position where defense of her person or others' is necessitated. If such occurs, then perhaps she is no lady at all.~~

—*Lady Druthers's Guide to Perfect Deportment and Etiquette*

One's reticule cannot only be stylish and perfect for holding one's valuables, it can also serve as an excellent ~~weapon~~ on the off chance you need one.

Chapter Six

Holding her skirts aloft, Primrose marched a hard line back for the tavern, compelled by a renewed purpose of finding—and perhaps rescuing—Olympia.

Most people were heading deeper into the Gardens, and since she was going against the flow of traffic, she walked along the edge of the main row, passing lanes that intersected the wide path. These cross paths were little better than alleyways running along between taverns and other establishments.

Prim glanced behind her. Man-boy, or Jacob, followed, looking rather grumpy with his unsmiling lips. He had lost his friends, too. It made sense that he would return to the place he had last seen them. She faced forward again, telling herself it was no concern of hers.

She was almost to the tavern now. The front doors yawned open. Even from several yards away she could see that it was nearly deserted inside, with only staff remaining to sweep and pick up the mess. No sight of Olympia in the vicinity. *Blast it!*

Primrose stopped and glanced around the row again, scanning the faces of strangers going about their merriment. Frustration bubbled up inside her chest.

Where was her friend? What was she to do?

She had enough coin in her reticule to get herself home, but they had arrived here together. Primrose did not want to depart without her friend. That felt . . . wrong. And she did not think Olympia would leave without her.

She could not imagine the awfulness of returning home to find Olympia still missing. What would she tell her Mrs. Zaher?

No. She would not leave this place without her. Oh why hadn't they discussed what to do if they became separated?

Jacob had almost caught up to her when a pair of men suddenly stepped out from one of the cross lanes in front of him. For a moment, she thought his friends had found him and she felt a stab of envy, wishing she were the one being reunited with hers. Then she realized these men were not dressed in a manner befitting companions of a gentleman. They were dressed shabbily, with patches in their worn and dirty garments.

She gasped when one of them, a lad with a wild mop of curls sticking out from his absurdly large top hat, abruptly brandished a dagger whilst the other lad grabbed and shoved Jacob violently off the main row and into the alley from which they'd emerged.

A quick glance around revealed no other passersby had noticed Jacob being seized so roughly.

No one except Primrose.

She was the only one who had witnessed the ambush.

She hesitated a moment, biting on the inside of her cheek fretfully.

A boisterous group of gentleman approached. She waved at them desperately. "Help! Help! Someone has . . ."

They continued walking, paying her no heed.

With an unladylike mutter, she surged forward, determined to do something.

Jacob had saved her from being trampled. Even if he had displeased her with his thoughtless remarks, helping him was the least she could do. She owed him that.

Of course, she had no plan.

She approached the mouth of the alley and peered around the corner in time to see the two lads toss him to the ground.

Jacob was not to be subdued, however.

He was quick on his feet, vaulting back up, fists ready, striking one of his attackers with surprising speed.

Naturally, they did not care for that.

The footpads knocked him back down. He rolled, avoiding their fists. One of the lads finally managed to seize him and to forage through his jacket, on the hunt for his pocketbook.

Jacob would not give up the fight, however. He twisted like a slippery eel, doing his best to evade the ruffian's hands.

The glint of a dagger flashed in the darkness and she reacted without thought.

She jumped into the alley, brandishing her reticule and crying out, "Halt there! Unhand him! I've called the Watch!"

A lie, of course, but she hoped the bluff would frighten them away.

The lads froze for a fraction of a moment, and then they bolted—the need for self-preservation prevailing as they scurried like rats on a sinking ship. They forgot all about the man whose pockets they were busy pilfering, fear of Newgate winning over their greed.

Their feet beat a loud retreat as they fled out the opposite end of the alley. Primrose rushed to where Jacob was crumpled on the ground. She bent over and grasped his arm.

"Are you terribly injured?" She assessed him worriedly, her fingers flexing over his sleeve.

He grunted and lifted himself to his feet. She tried to assist him, distrusting that he wasn't truly hurt. She had seen the footpads strike him at least once and she doubted that he was unscathed.

"Jacob?" she pressed, her concern for him overriding decorum.

Yes, she'd just used his Christian name.

"I could have handled that myself, you know."

"Oh. Indeed?" Had she not insisted the very same thing to him?

"Indeed," he agreed.

She gave him an arch look and began to slide her hand off his arm, but he stopped her, seizing her fingers. Startled, she looked down at where his hand covered hers, where they were connected. Prim sucked in a breath and held it.

Butterflies danced in her chest, swooping down into her belly. She had never felt a boy's hand before. Not without gloves between them.

Everything slowed as she gazed down at where their hands joined.

His hand was much larger, the back of it broad and strong, lightly veined and sprinkled with hairs. *Competence.* That was the word that floated across her mind. These weren't the hands of an old man, like Begonia's husband. Not the lily-white, slight hands of Violet's betrothed. These were the hands of a competent and vital young man. Not a boy.

Prim winced. There was really no sense in comparing Jacob to any of the very few gentlemen in her life, because he would never be a gentleman in her life. Not beyond this moment. Not beyond this night. He was so far afield from *her.* She might as well be swooning over the moon.

Jacob's hand flexed over hers, enveloping her hand in a firm, warm grasp. It was most disconcerting. True, she had initiated the contact, but it still sent a bolt of awareness skittering through her.

Her gaze lifted back to his, and she felt pulled in, drawn into the compelling darkness of his eyes, causing her stomach to flutter anew. She fought to quell the sensation. She'd best not come to expect things like flutters. No good could come of it. Only heartache and disappointment.

Matches were made for practicality, not because of things like flutters. Mama had lectured on that point too many times to count. Along with the warning not to expect emotion or sentimentality from a future husband. According to her mother, it was not in a man's disposition, as they were far too concerned with masculine pursuits.

And why was she thinking of matches anyway? She was not

in one of the gothic romances she purchased from the local bookshop and then hid from Mama. Mama blamed such books for filling Prim's head with rubbish.

And it was not as though Jacob was a viable marital prospect.

Even so . . . she was certain her mother had been wrong. Sentiment existed in Jacob. She was sure of it. There was something deep and indiscernible in his gaze. It was a far cry from detachment.

"Your hand is cold," he murmured.

Prim quickly slipped her hand out from under his, severing the contact as she stepped back, clearing her throat as though that might help dislodge the lump that had taken residence there. "You are certain you are well?"

"I am unharmed. Just a little dirty." He straightened, brushing off his dark jacket. "I suppose I do owe you thanks for your quick thinking."

"Oh it seemed the obvious thing to do."

"Obvious?" His lips quirked. "For you, perhaps. Not many others would have done the same. It was brave and daring. I'm beginning to suspect you are quite fearless."

Warm pleasure spread through Prim at the compliment. She had never considered herself fearless before. She didn't know if it was true. Stuck most of her life in the family nursery, she had not been given too many opportunities. Perhaps this night was her test.

"Those footpads . . . they struck you." She motioned in the direction the scoundrels had fled and then looked back to him in concern. "Several times."

"They were more concerned with finding my pocketbook

than doing me any significant injury." He lightly touched his jaw and gave it a flex, as though verifying this fact for himself. "I've endured far greater roughhousing in my years at Eton."

She released a nervous little laugh. Eton? His family must indeed have deep pockets.

"I am relieved you are well. Perhaps you are the one in need of a chaperone?"

He blinked. "Me?"

"Yes." She nodded, smiling in amusement. "It seems Vauxhall can be dangerous. Even for strapping young men."

He stared at her uncertainly before smiling slowly in return. "Perhaps I do need a chaperone," he allowed, his voice a little deeper. "Are you volunteering for the position?"

Warmth flushed her face at his teasing. "Oh. I . . . uh—"

"Since you have proven yourself so very adept at saving my life."

She laughed lightly, an edge of nervousness dancing along her spine. "And now we're even. Although I don't think your life was seriously in jeopardy."

He leveled those mesmerizing dark eyes on her. They were like deep seas, ready to pull her under. "Perhaps we should remain together? Just until we find our friends?"

"Oh, um . . . I don't . . ."

He angled his head. "I promise not to get your nose out of joint. Er, again."

"So you're acknowledging your earlier rudeness then?"

He scratched his head. "I was perhaps a spot judgmental."

"A spot?"

"Perhaps more."

"Let's try arrogant and bossy."

"I promise I won't be any of those things with you."

"Hmm. Is that possible?"

"What mean you?"

"I thought they might be inherent to those blessed with wealth and privilege?" He went to Eton. It was safe to say he was no pauper, even if he didn't have a title.

"Now who is being judgmental?"

She snorted at that, the sound part choke and part laughter.

"Come now," he coaxed. "Don't you want to make certain I'm not accosted again? What shall I do without you at my side for protection?"

"Are you mocking me? Because I *did* save you."

He flattened a hand against his chest in outrage. "Me? I would never." His gaze turned serious. "What say you? Shall we look out for each other and search for our friends together?"

She gave a slow nod. "Very well, my l—" She stopped herself with a wince.

She could not know with any certainty if the footpads had attacked him because they overheard her address him so formally, but it seemed advisable to heed him and not do so again, even in jest.

"Jacob," she amended, ignoring the little thrill she felt at the intimate sound of his name on her lips.

He smiled slowly and it was devastating what it did to her— how could she feel hot and cold all at once? "And what shall I call you, my brave rescuer?" he murmured in that warm, deep voice that brought to mind crackling fires and hot chocolate.

He could be charming when he chose and it was quite a

turnabout from before. That felt dangerous and important to remember. She did not need to lose her head over him.

"Primrose." She could not bring herself to divulge her surname. "Prim," she volunteered, surrendering her name to him. It truly felt that way. A surrender of sorts. A surrender to this intimacy that seemed to have sprouted so quickly between them.

She could remind herself to keep her head. She could fight back the flutters.

But that didn't change the reality of her circumstances. She was wandering about Vauxhall with a charming man who appeared to be a skilled flirt.

Every girl who was ever compromised probably felt the same way at one time. She would be careful and try not to do anything she later regretted.

"Primrose," he echoed, as though tasting her name on his lips. "Fitting. It suits you."

The heat in her face only intensified. "My mother has an interest in floriculture." One of the few things aside from shopping and gossip and marrying off her daughters that held her interest. "She named all her daughters after her favored flowers."

"Ah . . . you must have a sister named Lily."

"Surprisingly, no."

"Ah." He nodded. "She didn't name one of your sisters after the corpse flower, I hope."

She let loose a short bark of laughter. "There is a corpse flower?"

"Indeed. Smells like a rotting animal."

"Oh dear. No. I do not have a sister named . . . Corpse."

"Well, that is a good thing." He gestured for them to depart the alley. She accepted his proffered arm, nestling her hand in the crook of his elbow.

Together, they stepped back out onto the main row, leaving the murk behind. Instantly she felt more at ease under the glow of lamplight.

They both looked left and right as though they might spot their friends. People strolled and bustled about, but no one she recognized.

His gaze settled on her face. "No sight of them." One of his shoulders lifted in a fatalistic half shrug. "Do you see your friend?"

She shook her head. "No. I don't see Olympia anywhere. She's wearing a bright yellow gown."

"Ah. Hard to miss, I imagine."

"Quite so," she agreed.

"Well. I am certain they are walking about looking for us at this very moment." He gave her an encouraging smile.

Gone was the surly man from earlier. She rather liked this smiling version of him. There was not a great amount of smiling in her home, and she couldn't help thinking how very much she liked his quick and ready grin.

She nodded, hoping he was correct. "I am certain, too."

"Then it is just us."

Us.

Primrose and a handsome young man. It was something she could never have dreamed up, even in her most far-fetched fantasies. And she did have those. Fantasies aplenty. There was always ample time for daydreaming when left to her devices, as she was most days (and most evenings). She had spent many an afternoon with a book half-read in her lap, gazing out the window, envisioning all the things she might do once she turned ten and six.

She could never have even fantasized this current reality.

A thrilling little shiver raced down her spine as the word *us* echoed through her mind. She should not feel so delighted at the prospect of them together. She should feel only worry for Olympia. Her friend was out there alone. Although Olympia was a most capable young lady. Her mother didn't keep her sequestered inside the house like a pet bird in its cage. She'd lived abroad in several different places, spoke multiple languages, and was so much more experienced and worldly than Primrose. Her friend always had a clever rejoinder. Olympia always knew what to do and say in any given situation.

There was consolation in that, at least.

They strolled down the row into the deepening night. "Have you any idea where your friend might have gone?" he asked. "Did you talk of something you wanted to see following the tavern?"

"Ah. Yes!" Prim nodded. Why had she not thought of that before? "I mentioned the acrobats to her!"

His expression brightened. "Well, I know where they are. Come along. It's this way."

No true gentleman would soil his gloves with trade.

—*Lady Druthers's Guide to
Perfect Deportment and Etiquette*

*There's something very attractive
about a man who is unafraid of
doing the work that needs
to be done.*

Chapter Seven

A crowd had gathered and it was difficult to see through the mass of bodies.

"Are you certain we are in the right place?" Prim asked, craning her neck in the hopes of obtaining a glimpse at what everyone was watching.

"Yes. Come, this way." He led her up a small knoll, winding through observers to reach the top. When they arrived at the peak, they turned and looked down at the acrobats. A cheerful tune played from nearby flutists whilst a trio of men tossed flaming batons with great skill.

It was impressive. Prim feared they were going to set their faces on fire at any moment, but they managed to remain unscathed.

She clapped her hands in delight when they started tossing the flaming batons back and forth to each other. "They are quite the marvel, are they not?" she asked, transfixed, unable to look away from the performers.

Her mouth fell wide in wonder as one of the acrobats arched his body, bending backward at the waist as he brought a baton with a peg at its center to his mouth and bit down on the peg.

"He's a regular contortionist!" she exclaimed. "Incredible!"

"It is a sight," he murmured beside her.

Something in his voice, a softness, caught her attention. She turned to find him staring at her, not the acrobats. He was studying *her*, his deep eyes tracking over her features, seeing everything, all the many spots Mama loathed. Although the way he was looking at her . . . she did not think he found them so loathsome.

Or perhaps she was imagining things? Perhaps she was seeing something in his eyes, feeling an electric charge in the air that weren't there?

The crowd gasped and she looked back at the performers.

One of the other acrobats lit both ends of a baton on fire and then he started spinning it like a giant pinwheel above his face. Astonished, she applauded as the flaming baton spun.

Jacob's voice intruded on her enjoyment of the outrageous spectacle. "Do you see your friend?"

"Oh." She turned away from the wondrous scene with a stab of guilt, lowering her hands.

Of course. Her gaze scanned the rapt faces of onlookers. She should be searching for Olympia. Her purpose here was not to be entertained. It was to find her friend, so that she and Jacob might go about their evening. Separately.

After a few moments of scanning the faces gathered around

her, she shook her head. "No, I don't see her. Do you see your friends?"

He looked out at the assemblage. "No."

She crossed her arms and rubbed them as though the pleasant summer evening were suddenly cold. She continued to scan the revelers, hoping any of the dark-haired ladies, or any flash of canary yellow, might turn out to be her friend and save her from this strange, swelling awkwardness with Jacob.

"Perhaps we should continue our search elsewhere?" he suggested.

She nodded and accepted his arm as he guided her down the knoll, casting one last look toward the acrobats.

"Jacob! Is that you?"

He stiffened for a moment and then continued walking, his pace quickening. Clearly, he'd heard the greeting, but would feign otherwise.

The bearer of that voice was not to be deterred, however. The woman called over the clapping and cheering of the crowd as the acrobats moved on to climbing each other in order to form an impressive triangle with their bodies.

"You there! Do you hear me?"

With a mutter, he stopped. Shooting Prim an apologetic glance, he turned with her on his arm to face the individual.

"Ah. Lady Kettering," he greeted as a woman around Prim's mother's age approached. A much younger pair of gentleman flanked her sides.

Lady Kettering. A noblewoman whose name Prim had read often in the scandal rags was standing before Primrose now. As Prim had read every book in her family's limited library, she

was happy to browse whatever written words crossed her path—
including the scandal sheets. Honestly, it was no chore. Certainly, she could not be too choosy when it came to her reading
material, and, wrong or right, she actually enjoyed the sala-
cious content.

That was how she knew that Lady Kettering was a widow
often seen about Town on the arm of one gentleman or another.
Usually not the same man, thus explaining why she was so frequently featured in the gossip rags.

Lady Kettering dismissed Prim with a quick scan, looking
her over and then flicking her gaze back to Jacob. Prim shifted
awkwardly on her feet. She wanted to shrink into a speck, and
disappear altogether, but then she caught herself. *No.* No, she
should not want to vanish simply because she was embarrassed
at this woman's dismissal. Prim was used to being rather invisible at home, but this was different. She was not at home and
Lady Kettering was not a member of her family.

She refused to feel invisible here too.

The woman might have been around her mother's age, but
there the similarity ended. She wore a gown of deep scarlet
trimmed in black lace. It was much too tight in the chest. The
square neckline cut deep into the creamy swells of her breasts,
carving into the mounds right above the nipples. Prim feared
that one sneeze or laugh, and the woman would be exposed
before all and sundry.

The lady slapped Jacob in his chest with her large fan. "Oh
la, if it isn't our handsome recluse. Ah!" She glanced to each of
her companions. "Can you believe it, lads?"

They replied almost in unison. "I cannot believe it."

"Good evening, my lady," Jacob greeted.

"It's very nice to see you out and about. You did not attend my salon last week." She frowned in petulance and slapped him yet again with her fan. "You naughty man."

Prim wasn't too familiar with the flirtations between men and women, but she had a suspicion she was witnessing that very thing now, which was a strange thing indeed, as the woman reminded her of a more flamboyant Mama, and Prim could not imagine her mother flirting with anyone, much less a man young enough to be her son.

"Your mother said you were in the country. Fishing." She laughed then and Prim eyed her bosom in fear, hoping she did not explode from her dress.

The young men at her side joined her in laughter as though cued in by Lady Kettering's guffaws. She cackled so heartily that the artificial beauty mark on her upper cheek quivered and fell off her face. Primrose stared down at the ground as though she might see it in the dark grass.

The woman sobered, continuing in a chiding tone. "'Fishing,' I said, 'certainly our Jacob knows better than to eschew the delights of the season to fish?'"

"I was fishing in the Lake District for a spell with some friends."

If Prim had any doubts before, they were put to rest. This well-heeled young man was gentry, and perhaps more. Perhaps even aristocracy. He took fishing trips to the Lake District with friends. He attended Eton. His mother and Lady

Kettering were intimates. He was an acquaintance of Lady Kettering, a noblewoman who was frequently splashed all over the papers.

Just who exactly was he? She would have asked if she did not fear he would require the same honesty from her.

"Ah, the Lake District. Such lovely country . . . for a short time, at any rate. Then the wonders of London beckon. Or Bath perhaps. But the country?" She shuddered dramatically. "How could one stay there longer than a night or two? I'd perish of boredom. Would you not, lads?" She looked to her companions.

"Indeed, indeed," they quickly agreed, and Prim could not help wondering if they shared a brain.

"Well!" The lady clapped her hands merrily, her gloves muffling the sound. "So happy to see you're back in Town. I'm hosting a dinner next week. I'll send round an invitation now that I know you've returned." Her gaze drifted to Primrose in final acknowledgment. "You're welcome to bring your friend here." Her rouged lips curled as she made the offer and Prim knew it was the furthest thing from sincere. On sight, it seemed, the lady did not like her—as though she sniffed out that her pedigree was less than desirable. "I do not believe I've caught your name, m'dear." She looked Primrose over critically, waiting with an air of impatience.

"I . . . ah . . ." She did not know what to say.

She knew what *not* to say, which was her real name.

Except she had not prepared a false name to supply, and she could only stammer foolishly.

"This is Fiona. My Scottish cousin." Jacob had no problem thinking on his feet. The lie tripped of his tongue with ease.

She would almost have believed him—if she did not know the truth.

"Oh!" Lady Kettering's manner changed instantly. "What a pleasure to meet you." She stepped forward to press a wet, effusive kiss to Prim's cheek. She reeked of spirits. "You must come to dinner with your cousin next week." Yes, she was decidedly friendlier now. "I've the most brilliant French chef. Horrible temperament—what can you expect from a Frenchman?—but his pastries are ambrosia."

The woman didn't take a breath to give Prim room to speak. No sooner had she stepped back than she was saying, "Scotland has such splendid hunting. My late husband always said that if you wanted boar, then you must venture to Scotland for it."

Primrose resisted mentioning that wild boars were purported to be on the decline in Scotland, and already extinct in England. She'd read that in a journal in her family library. Perhaps this lady's late husband was part of the cause for that, she thought wryly.

"And how long will you be in Town?" she asked of Prim.

"Och, only a fortnight, sad tae say," she replied in a reasonably impressive Scottish brogue.

Jacob arched an eyebrow and gave a slight nod of approval, and she tried not to feel too pleased by that.

"Ah! Splendid! Well, perhaps you can join us in the park tomorrow. Or for afternoon tea? You needn't wait until next week's dinner, m'dear."

She spoke as though it were agreed upon already that she and Jacob would attend her dinner party.

"We will have to verify our calendar, my lady. My secretary

has our schedule, but I think we already have a prior commitment." He squeezed Prim's shoulder. "My cousin is in high demand during her stay."

He really was an exceptional liar.

"How disappointing." Lady Kettering pouted. It was not a good look.

"Aye, verra disappointing," Primrose chimed, getting into the spirit of their ruse.

"Now if you will pardon us. We've lost one of our friends and we must locate her," Jacob quickly supplied.

"Oh dear." Lady Kettering scanned the grounds. "You best find her . . . you wouldn't want her to be dragged off onto one of the dark walks." She shared a meaningful look with her two cohorts, who each nodded grimly back. "We've heard many a tale of virtues lost there."

"Aye." One of the young men nodded. "I've heard of souls lost on the dark walks that have yet to surface."

Prim blinked. *They had never surfaced?* Were the dark walks some manner of vortex in to which one disappeared, never to emerge again? That was rather undesirable for a pleasure garden.

"Sound advice. We best hasten," Jacob intoned with a nod. "Good even'."

He took Prim's elbow once again, guiding her from the crowd gathered to watch the skilled acrobats.

"Well." Prim slid him a considering glance. "Lady Kettering. She seemed quite . . ."

"The dragon? Her children with the earl never reached adulthood and it's rumored she ate her young."

112

Primrose giggled even though she knew she should not. "You're awful."

He glanced down at her, that attractive face of his stoic until he caught sight of *her* face. Then he smiled. "I know."

"That's a terrible thing to say," she reprimanded.

"Yes," he agreed. "It is. I'm incorrigible . . . and Lady Kettering is someone I can't abide for longer than two sentences."

"That was much longer than two sentences. You managed."

"Indeed not. I'm most harmed, but I shall endeavor to recover."

They fell to silence as they left the acrobats behind.

The crowd thinned out as they walked deeper into the Gardens. The buildings and structures became fewer as well. Soon tall trees hemmed them in on either side of the lamp-lit row.

The quiet grew oppressive, almost suffocating.

"So . . ." She cleared her throat, continuing to scrutinize people they passed, hoping for a glimpse of Olympia. "Fiona? Scotland?"

He chuckled. "It was the first thing that popped in my mind."

His chuckle was a wonderful sound. Warm and as comforting as a sip of hot chocolate on a chilly morning.

"Will you go to her dinner party next week?"

"Oh no." He shook his head firmly. "That's not even in the realm of possibility."

"Well, that was quite emphatic of you."

"I am quite emphatic on the matter. Attending *ton* parties does not rank high in my priorities."

"You're fortunate you have a choice." She was quick to retort before she could think better of it.

She felt his gaze, long and intense, on the side of her face.

She stared straight ahead, refusing to let him see her features, fearful of what he might glimpse there.

"I've never thought of it like that before."

Of course he hadn't. When one had freedoms, one never considered what life would be like without them.

One didn't have to.

"So do you even fish?" she asked in a brighter tone, forcing levity back between them.

"On occasion. I enjoy the outdoors and sports. The Lake District is a favorite place of mine to visit. My mother, however, clings to this excuse, that I am away fishing, for whenever I am not present at events. I suppose she feels the need to provide an explanation." He shrugged.

"I take it that is often? That you are not present?"

He shrugged. "Often enough. I have my own pursuits."

She pursed her lips. He had his own pursuits—things aplenty to occupy him whilst she was forced to stay home. She blew out a disgusted breath. It shouldn't irk her, but it did.

"So what are these pursuits?" She couldn't suppress her curiosity. The only gentleman really in her life was her father, and he spent most of his days avoiding her mother. That seemed to be his chief occupation.

Following breakfast, Papa would take himself to his club, where he spent most of the day among other gentlemen conversing, playing cards, drinking, smoking cigars—all the leisurely activities of a gentleman. At times he even attended a lecture.

Papa had inherited a small country estate from his father.

That was where he'd grown up, frolicking and running along the Cliffs of Dover.

As Mama had no interest in country living, even in so picturesque a setting, she had convinced him to sell the property and relocate to London. A poor decision. At least when Papa had owned his country estate, he'd received rents from tenants. Now they lived off the ever-dwindling money from its sale.

Mama never approved of discussions having to do with money, or lack thereof, but Prim had listened in on Papa with his man from the bank. Their funds were on the decline even all those years ago.

Jacob spoke beside her. "Well, I'm required here some of the year. I have responsibilities and matters to attend to . . . and then there's my estate. It requires a great deal of attention in the day-to-day operation."

"You don't have people to manage it for you?" She could not see him elbows deep in ledgers or tilling the fields with laborers.

"I have a good staff, but I like to be involved. Work through the accounts, check over the fields myself, explore new developments in agriculture. My father always told me that a man who is blind to his affairs limits himself from greatness."

She'd always thought of the gentry as an indolent group, but he was painting a different picture. She swallowed, questioning everything she had ever been taught. According to Mama, gentlemen did not muddy their hands with labor. They had servants or staff for that. But he was not at all like that.

"You aspire to greatness?" she asked.

He looked a little uncomfortable at that question. "Let's just

say I aspire. My father was a great man. If I could be half as decent, I should feel gratified."

"He passed away?"

"A year next month."

To have so much responsibility thrust upon one so young, Prim could not fathom that. "My condolences."

"He'd been sick. It was a relief to see him out of pain."

She nodded.

They turned onto another path. Not a dark walk. Rather, this row was still wide and well-lit by strategically placed lanterns.

"And what of you and your family? You mentioned sisters. How many do you have?"

"Three."

"So there are three others like you? All bearing floral names?"

She laughed slightly at that. "Suffice it to say my sisters are nothing like me, beyond our names."

"No?"

She nodded. "Not even in the slightest."

He nodded back, the motion slow. "Intriguing. You are the anomaly."

"Black sheep," she admitted.

"Ah, a venerable position in any family."

She half-winced, half-smiled. "I try to do it justice."

He laughed lightly. "Sneaking off to Vauxhall will do the trick." He paused before adding, "You said you were all named after flowers?"

"Yes. There is my eldest sister Begonia. She is married with children. Violet is betrothed and Aster is yet unmarried," she recounted.

116

"Ah, a dwindling numbers of debutantes in your house. It's down to you and Aster."

"Nothing is expected of me until Aster has become formally betrothed."

"You have a reprieve then. And that is . . . good? Or disappointing?" He looked at her expectantly and she wondered when had it suddenly become so comfortable to talk to him.

Their steps crunched over the loose pebbles on the cobbled path as they walked. Prim still kept her eye out for a flash of yellow. "I am in no haste to wed . . ." Especially as she now faced the fact that Mama would be the one largely making all the decisions when it came to who her suitors would be.

"That would make you very different from most debutantes of my acquaintance. They call the season the marriage mart for a reason, after all."

She knew her admission could be seen as unconventional. Sometimes Prim wished she had a better grasp of what she wanted for her life. If she were more like Begonia and Violet, her life would be far simpler. "As I said, I am *the* black sheep."

"I am an only child," he volunteered. "Unless my mother ever decides to remarry. She is young enough." He shrugged. "Younger than I am when she had me."

"You think that possible?"

"It's doubtful she would give up being my father's widow to be the wife of another, lesser man, at least a lesser man by her estimation. Even gone, my father's legacy holds true, and still provides her with many advantages. She views her marriage as the greatest accomplishment of her life."

"I doubt that. There is you, her son. I'm certain you rank as

one of her greatest accomplishments." She wrinkled her nose. "And what if she met someone? Lesser man or not, what if she fell in love again? She would not consider setting aside her widowhood then?"

"Such a romantic thought, but no. My mother would consider marriage to another man only if he possessed wealth and position greater than her own. And that seems unlikely."

Again with the implication that he was quite high up the ladder of Society. She tamped down on her curiosity. It would be rude to inquire just *what* and *who* he was. She would not define him by his position.

He was Jacob. For tonight, that was the only thing that mattered.

He laughed lightly. "You must think my mother a wretched snob."

"Oh no. Not . . . wretched."

He laughed. "Just a snob then?"

She pulled a face. "Is she not?" He'd just admitted she would remarry again only if it were, presumably, to someone like a duke. Or a prince. Or . . . a *king*.

He dragged a hand through his dark hair, sending all the lush strands into wild disarray. "She is exactly that."

It dawned on her that he had likely met such people in his life. Dukes and princes and kings were probably real to him and not merely people he read about in the gossip sheets.

She marveled at that. This young man beside her had likely met the same king she read about in the papers — the king who was overly fond of his drink, and who was often embroiled in one love affair or another.

She shook her head. He was of another world, the gulf between them wide.

Except for tonight. No gulf existed as they walked side by side in easy companionship.

"It must be nice to have siblings." His voice pulled her from her thoughts.

She lifted one shoulder. "It can . . . complicate your life." That seemed the kindest way to explain it.

"Complicate? How?"

"But I am certain you don't want to hear the long and tedious drama of my family?" And certainly it was not acceptable to discuss such things with him. Not that anything about this night was acceptable thus far, but she needed to remember they were veritable strangers. Also, talking about her family disheartened her.

Their path converged with another and the foot traffic picked up as people poured in alongside them. Still no sight of canary yellow.

"Where is everyone going?" she asked.

Clearly there was a popular destination ahead. To seemingly confirm this, a distant roar of applause went up.

"I am not certain. Shall we investigate?"

It stood to reason that any place attracting a crowd was worth exploring.

She nodded, and they fell in with the current of people. Ahead, Primrose noted several dozen moving toward a rotunda.

"What is in there?" She pointed at the wooden structure.

Jacob followed her gaze and frowned, slowing them to a stop. "Oh. You don't want to go in there." He glanced around

them as though looking for some place more appealing to take them.

She smiled ruefully, now fully enticed. "Well, now of course I do. What is it?"

He stopped with a sigh and looked toward the building. "Animal-baiting."

"Animal-baiting?"

He nodded. "Yes. Blood sport."

She frowned. "Animal-baiting . . . but that doesn't sound very sporting." A sport, in her mind, involved people engaged in a game, in an activity of some sort.

"It's not," Jacob agreed.

Her gaze roamed over the people passing through the double doors of the rotunda. Most were gentlemen, but there were ladies, too. All wore faultlessly benign expressions as they flowed through the entrance in a steady wave. They did not appear as though they were engaging in anything untoward. They all looked perfectly normal.

Perfectly normal people attending what must be a normal entertainment. Why else would so many flock to it? It couldn't be anything too terrible.

She recalled reading that animal-baiting had been greatly popular during the Elizabethan era. Queen Elizabeth herself had been a great proponent, and she was one of Primrose's favorite historical figures.

There must be something worthy in it if the venerable Good Queen Bess had patronized such games . . . and if so many people flocked to watch it now.

"I would like to see," she declared.

A flicker of a cringe passed over his face. "I don't think that's a good idea."

"It's a popular event, clearly. What if your friends are there? What if Olympia's inside?" At this point, who knew where their friends could be? Perhaps Olympia was also following crowds and searching for her, just as Prim was? "Should we not go simply to search for them? If for no other reason than that?"

He sighed and she heard the beginning of surrender in the sound. He was relenting. She needed to push just a little bit more.

"It can't be that bad," she reasoned. "Why else would so many people want to—"

"I still do not think it a good idea."

She leveled a cajoling look at him. "You're not going to attempt to direct me once more, are you? I thought we agreed there'd be no more judgments."

He snorted. "Does this mean I must fall in with *all* your schemes and demands? What if *I* don't wish to see it?"

"You can come here or *anywhere* whenever you want and *not* see it," she pointed out. "Permit me this." She would never come here again, after all. At least not any time soon.

"Is that going to be your argument for everything tonight?"

"Perhaps. Is it working?"

He groaned and looked with curled lips toward the rotunda again.

She released his arm. "You mustn't do anything you do not wish, Jacob." Lifting her chin, she advanced to the rotunda, leaving him behind . . . even as she hoped he would follow. She walked a straight line, refusing to look back. It was a gamble.

A moment later he was beside her. "You're going to be the death of me, Prim. I haven't known you a day and you seem able to twist me around your finger."

She grinned. "I'm saving you from tedium."

"And pushing me straight to Bedlam."

She laughed, delighted, and wondered how she would ever return to her normal, monotonous life in Belgrave Square after this. Days stuck indoors, rereading the same books in their library whilst her family went about their many diversions. Without her.

How would she return to that after a night like this? After knowing him?

Spots on a lady's face announce that she has no care for her complexion. Society might then wonder what else she holds in so little regard.

> —*Lady Druthers's Guide to*
> *Perfect Deportment and Etiquette*

Why must one's outer beauty matter so much more than one's mind and heart?

Chapter Eight

They passed through the building's double doors and plunged into the darker interior that smelled overwhelmingly of body odor, cologne . . . and a horse's stall? Animal musk and waste. She remembered them from the one time she had visited the countryside.

A few years ago, she and Aster had accompanied Papa to call on an old friend in Kent. The two men had ensconced themselves in the library with their brandy whilst she and Aster explored the farm. Of course they had found their way to the barn, where a stable lad had shown them a tabby cat and her litter of newborn kittens.

Aster discovered she was allergic to cats on that day. Red splotches erupted on her skin, and her eyes almost swelled shut. But Prim had settled onto a comfortable spot among the hay, petting kittens, with the tang of animal musk, the stink of manure, and the aroma of loamy earth filling her nostrils.

She recalled that day, that moment, so precisely because she remembered thinking country living might agree with her. She might be considered a Londoner, but she had reveled in the brief taste of her father's youth.

She had wished to no avail that Papa had never sold his family estate, so that she could have lived in Kent. She would have had the vast countryside to roam and explore instead of being left on her own in their cramped town house so often.

Perhaps that memory reassured her, stirring something inside her while also comforting her as she and Jacob entered the building, bodies pressing on every side of them. She did not think she had ever been in such close confines with so many people before.

It grew only more crowded the farther they advanced up the narrow ramp. At the top of the incline, they came to a stop and peered down at a circular pit below. A pole was staked at the center of it, the dirt around it stained in what she could only surmise to be blood.

She looked up and observed the raised arena surrounding the pit. The rotunda was already full to the brim with people seated on tiered benches. Eagerness hummed in the air. She could taste it, along with something else. A sour bitterness, like metal in her mouth.

It wasn't pleasant and it gave her pause.

Someone bumped into them from behind, jolting Prim forward.

"Move along, would ye?" a voice snapped.

Jacob clasped her elbow and ushered her out of the way, casting a glare at the offending gentleman.

The lady at the man's side tittered, slapping his arm lightly with her swinging reticule. "Have pity. The lass looks a bit green," she said loud enough for Primrose to hear.

The man who bumped her cast Prim a scornful glance, wrinkling his bulbous and veined nose as though he caught wind of something disagreeable—something other than the less-than-fresh air inside the rotunda. "Children should not be permitted in the Gardens. Especially not at any of the fights."

"Indeed," the woman agreed. "Mamas should keep a tighter rein on their offspring. What is this world coming to when children are let loose from the nursery?"

Children!

"Oh." Prim puffed out an indignant breath. Her lips worked to let loose more incoherent outraged sputtering.

Girls her age were oft married. Not that she wanted to be married just yet. It was simply the unfortunate consequence—and usually the goal—of coming out in Society. It was difficult to differentiate between the two things. But if females her age were permitted to be wives and mothers, then she should be allowed an evening in the Gardens without public censure. Young men her age were allowed to go places and do all manner of things. Her indignation burned hotter as she contemplated the unfair disparity between men and women. Perhaps the thing that was most unfair about it was that it was likely not going to change any time soon.

How different her life would be if she had been born a boy. Besides the obvious differences of anatomy, she would be permitted about Town with Papa and allowed inside his club and to the gaming halls he liked to frequent. She would indulge in spirits and cigars in the library with all the gentlemen after dinner, not forced to do needlework with the rest of the ladies.

She'd always wondered what the men talked about in the library. She imagined the gentlemen discussed matters of philosophy, politics, and art. Perhaps she was being fanciful, though, as her father wasn't much of a conversationalist at any rate, and his friends seemed equally boring. How much could one really say about the taste of port?

Jacob again distracted her from her reverie by speaking quickly near her ear. "This isn't for you. Nor me. Let us leave this—"

"No," she protested, shaking her head stubbornly. She wasn't a child. Despite everyone's insistence on treating her like one. Adults did this. Whatever "this" was. She could too. "I can do this."

I can be an adult.

Of course she could.

There were easily over a hundred people here, with more filing in by the second. Evidently this was a popular form of entertainment. She would discover for herself whether it was for her or not. Jacob, well-meaning though he might be, did not need to make any decisions for her.

"Very well." With his lips set in an unyielding line, he settled his hand at the small of her back and together they turned from the ramp and started their ascent up into the raised tiers.

They climbed several rows up until they found a bench with enough room for both of them. They were forced to sit close; Jacob on one side and a random older gentleman on the other side of her. The gentleman looked down at her once, his expression mildly annoyed at having to make room for her. Then he turned to his friend beside him and they began discussing how much to wager on the upcoming match.

She turned to Jacob. "When do you think it will begin—" The rotunda suddenly went wild with cheers, cutting off her question. Prim sat up straighter on her bench to better peer down into the arena.

A trio of men entered with a ragged-looking bear tethered between them. She'd seen bears in illustrations and read about them in books, but she had never observed a bear in the flesh. She had thought them to be more impressive than this poor creature. His fur was dingy and matted in uneven snarls. In several places the fur was missing altogether, revealing patches of scarred pink flesh.

Each man held a long crop that he used to direct the bear, prodding and striking it. She winced with each blow.

A sinking sensation started in her belly and she leaned closer to Jacob to say over the din, "The bear looks . . ."

"Pitiable?" Jacob supplied.

She nodded, transfixed as they secured the beast by a hind leg to the stake in the center of the pit. The bear slumped there, its face lifting to scent the air. Otherwise, it did not move. It seemed . . . defeated.

"Yes, he doesn't strike me as very . . . spry," she added, fighting the mad urge to jump down into the pit and herd the bear to safety herself.

"He's blind."

"Blind?"

"Aye. They blind the bears."

She looked at him sharply. His grim expression told her he was not jesting.

She glanced around them, expecting to see other horrified spectators. Not so. Much to her disappointment, she observed everyone eagerly placing wagers, not the slightest bit dismayed at the sight of the wretched creature below.

Shrill barking filled the air, preceding the arrival of the dogs.

Prim's skin went clammy cold in premonition. Jacob was right. She should not have come here.

The frenzied energy in the air only heightened. Even the bear grew more agitated, no longer slumped in place, but standing on all fours, alert and pacing as much as the tether permitted him.

He sensed the danger and twisted his neck, pulling at his tether as though he could break himself free.

She, too, sensed it.

Even if the danger wasn't coming for her. She felt ill. Prim pressed a hand against her roiling stomach, willing the queasiness to abate.

"How is this a sport?" she muttered. "It's cruel."

He'd warned her. He had. But Prim hadn't listened.

If this kind of entertainment signified she was now an adult, then perhaps staying a child was for the best. She did not like it and she no longer wanted to be here.

The crowd grew more frenzied, animals themselves, hollering, shoving at each other to have their bets heard and recorded.

The dogs arrived, spilling into the pit in a wild tumble of snapping jaws, kept at bay by the men holding their tethers.

Their masters themselves were full of vitriol, shouting at

each other when the dogs' leads got tangled, and then there was no keeping the dogs off each other. The bear was forgotten as the men and dogs all became embroiled, one cursing, howling pile of bodies, human and canine.

The rolling in her stomach only intensified as one of the men went down with flailing arms and a dog turned on him, sinking its very large teeth into his arm.

Nearby, the bear, even though blind, sat on its back legs as though enjoying the demonstration. He cocked his head as if he could understand everything happening based on sound alone.

"Serves these men right," Jacob muttered.

Blood sprayed across the pit.

"Oh!" Sour bile rose up in Prim's throat. She covered her mouth with a trembling hand and turned her head to the side, burying it in Jacob's shoulder, but not before she caught a glimpse of his face. He looked a bit green about the gills, too.

"You daft little fool," he growled, and she knew she deserved that. He'd tried to keep her from coming here, but she wouldn't listen.

Grabbing her hand, Jacob pulled her up from the bench and down the steps and ramp, bustling her out of the arena.

She sucked in a fresh breath, glad to be away from the smell and sight of all that blood.

Out of sight but not out of mind, for the shouts of the fight followed after them. A roll of cheers went up from the building. That savagery was still happening in there. Among the animals. Among the men.

"How is that civilized?" The words choked from her throat.

The bile still rode high in her chest, threatening to spill free. She made a terrible gagging sound as she fought to hold it back.

He moved quickly, ushering her to a bench situated in front of the rotunda. "Don't torment yourself. There is naught you can do about it." He rubbed slow circles on her back. She could not even ponder the terrible inappropriateness of his touch, so intimate and familiar on her. Furthermore, she could not summon forth the will to protest, as she knew she should. Not with the contents of her stomach rushing up to her throat. There was no help for it. She couldn't rid herself of the image of spraying blood.

In humiliating fashion, she leaned over and retched, shaking and quivering like a leaf in a storm. Her mask chafed at her face. With a frustrated growl, she snatched it off and tossed it on the ground. Pressing her palms over her eyes and nose, she sighed at the welcoming coolness of her own touch. And there was the added benefit that her face was shielded from Jacob.

"There, there," he comforted, still rubbing her back.

Finished, she lifted her head and said rather pitifully, "This is the worst birthday."

His hand was there, ready before her with a handkerchief. She accepted it weakly, mortified. She had just retched in front of him, this handsome young nob. However did one recover from such a thing? *Could* she?

Pressing his handkerchief to her lips, she inhaled and caught the faint scent of sandalwood. "Apologies," she muttered against the soft linen.

"Nonsense. No apology necessary. Better now?"

She nodded, lowering the handkerchief from her lips. Better

physically, at least. Her spirit would require a little more time to heal.

She lifted her miserable gaze to his face. He was waiting, his attention fixed to her. "It's not over yet," he murmured.

"What isn't?" she asked warily. Did he know something she did not? Was she not done being sick in front of him?

"Your birthday. It's not over yet."

"Oh." She huffed a little. "You think it will get better?" In this moment, she possessed little faith in that.

He smiled that slow grin that made her stomach flip and coaxed a smile from her. "I know it will."

And just like that Prim's faith was restored.

She flushed, and knew it had everything to do with that smile of his and the gravelly scrape of his voice. It felt like a tangible brush over her skin.

"You're terribly confident." Her voice trembled ever so slightly. She hoped that if he noticed the tremor, he attributed it to the upheaval of the last few minutes and not anything to do with his deep eyes and even deeper voice.

She felt like such a green girl. He was likely accustomed to droves of more sophisticated *women* who could converse intelligently with him without blushing and their voices cracking. Olympia would know how to behave and comport herself. Good heavens. *Olympia.* Where could she be?

"You've gone to great lengths to have a memorable night." Those deep eyes were as dark as the night surrounding them, both pinning her in place and pulling her in. "You shall have it. I promise you that."

~~Propriety entails modesty and restraint.~~
~~A lady should never make herself too memorable.~~
—*Lady Druthers's Guide to*
Perfect Deportment and Etiquette

Chapter Nine

His impassioned vow hummed between them. *You've gone to great lengths to have a memorable night. You shall have it. I promise you that.*

She considered that. Memorable it already was, but she wanted it to be magical too. She winced. That might be too much to hope. Retching in front of this man whose opinion somehow mattered to her was not the least bit enchanting.

"That is kind of you to say." She swallowed to wet her suddenly dry throat.

His eyes traveled over her face. After a moment, he whispered, "There you are."

She frowned, pressing the back of her hand to her clammy cheek. "What do you mean? Of course I'm here."

"No more hiding behind a mask. I can see you as I first did. The birthday girl from the tea shop." His finger reached out to

stroke down the bridge of her nose, triggering goose bumps up and down on her arms.

With a small shiver, she remembered. *Her mask.*

It was gone. *Drat!*

She'd cast her domino to the ground rather boldly and haphazardly with no thought to the consequences.

His touch didn't stop on her nose though.

Jacob's finger continued, gliding over to her cheek. His other fingers joined there and then she could scarcely breathe as the rough pads of his fingertips brushed over her skin, back and forth, back and forth, gentle as a brush stroke, eliciting all manner of sensations within Prim.

She fidgeted, shifting her weight. She should put the mask back on her face while she was in the gardens. Less risky with Redding, and heavens knew who else wandering about. And yet it felt good to have it off — even if that meant Jacob had an unfettered view of the unfortunate spots on her nose that Mama so bemoaned. The various creams and tinctures Mama would put on Prim's freckles in an attempt to be rid of them never worked — not that it stopped Mama from trying.

Jacob angled his head, his gaze lifting from her face to her hair. "I mean, with that hair your mask was not much of a disguise, but it's still nice to see your face again."

She looked down at her hands, wishing away the volley of nerves suddenly besetting her. "My hair is too . . . brazen." Mama had told her that plenty of times.

"Your hair is beautiful." The rejoinder came quickly. Forcefully.

Her gaze snapped up to his face and remained there, trapped in all that beautiful darkness.

Perhaps there was a bit of magic to the night after all.

Her lips parted to thank him for the compliment, but no sound escaped.

They did not speak. They simply stared at one another with his *magical* words between them and her pulse racing.

He cleared his throat and looked off somewhere in the distance. "Ah. Wait here one moment."

He left her on the bench and trotted over to a vendor. He spoke to the man and offered him a farthing in exchange for one of the several drinks and a biscuit available on his cart. Moments later, Jacob returned with a glass and biscuit in hand.

"Here." He held up the cup to her lips. "Drink this."

She sipped delicately at first, testing it. Once she recognized it as the ratafia she had liked so much at the tavern, she drank more greedily.

"Now have a bite of this," he directed.

She accepted the iced biscuit from him and took a bite. It was lemon and so tasty. She took several more bites, surprised that she had an appetite after what she just witnessed. Then again, it was well past the dinner hour.

She finished off the biscuit and the drink.

Feeling refreshed, she handed him back the cup with a murmured thanks.

"You are very kind to look after me," she added, dusting off her fingers.

Warmth spread through her now much calmer belly and it occurred to her, belatedly, that she should perhaps have not

consumed her drink so quickly. Especially on an empty stomach. She was unaccustomed to the effect of spirits, and she knew they influenced people in sometimes inappropriate ways. She needed to keep her wits about her.

She'd heard Mama tell Papa that Redding was a little too fond of his drink. Violet did not seem concerned on the matter — or at least she always defended him when Mama complained about it, insisting that he was only ever enjoying himself and there was no harm in that. On the occasions Primrose had been in Redding's company, no spirits had been served, but she'd had a flash of his face in the tavern earlier, flushed and ruddy, his eyes glassy, his laughter as loud as a braying mule's. Doubtlessly, he had been drinking then.

Indeed, somewhere tonight in these very Gardens he was well foxed, which was fortunate for her. It would be unlikely for him to recognize her if they crossed paths again.

She and Jacob sat on the bench for some moments, the sound of revelry within the Gardens a distant hum in the air.

She stared into the evening at the people strolling about, intent on their own leisure. "Those poor beasts. I don't understand why people take pleasure in such brutality."

"Not all people do."

She waved a hand toward the rotunda. "Well, there are many in there who are taking great pleasure."

"And many more who are not."

She shook her head. "I suppose I'm not so grown-up, after all."

"Don't consider yourself a child simply because you don't revel in animals being abused. Most people are not so cruel."

He turned on the bench and leaned slightly in without touching her, as though he was imbuing reassurance with his proximity. "There are other people like you who would get sickened at the sight of such brutality." He paused and then added, "'Gentleness is the antidote for cruelty.'"

She sent him a quick inquisitive look. "Plato?"

His nodded. "You know your Greek philosophizers?"

She shrugged, determined not to bask beneath what sounded like praise in his voice. "We've a few of his books in our library." And she had a great deal of time on her hands for reading.

"Not your typical reading for a young lady."

Typical? She bristled. "Is it not? And what would be *typical* reading for a young lady?"

"Oh." He blinked and shifted in discomfort. "I did not mean to offend. I merely—"

"You think I read only scandal rags and fashion plates? Is that the only material the female brain can manage?"

He let out a gust of breath and dragged a hand through his hair. "I did not mean to offend. I have no sisters, and my mother—" His voice faded.

She softened a little at the look crossing his face. It was there for only a moment. Just a flash of something vulnerable. "Your mother?" she prompted.

"Well, I wanted to say she doesn't read Greek philosophy, but then I don't really know her well enough to say."

Prim digested that for a moment, nodding slowly. She could accuse her mother of many things. But never could Prim claim she didn't *know* her.

Prim knew her almost too well. She knew all her faults and

all her strengths. Yes, she had to acknowledge that her mother had some good in her, too.

Mama might be overbearing and insensitive to the wishes of others, but her family was everything to her. She merely thought that her way was the best way and everyone else was wrong.

Jacob continued, "We're never in a room very long together, but I've never seen her read a book. Never seen one even in her vicinity. She has her friends and parties and many charities to occupy her. Mostly her parties. She lives for the season."

"You do not reside with your mother?"

"No." He shook his head. "When I'm in Town I stay at my own town house. She resides at the family residence in Mayfair."

They kept multiple homes in Town and in the country?

She knew it was the way of the very rich, of the *noblesse,* and she was more and more certain he could be counted in their ranks. The only close comparison she could make was with Violet's betrothed. Redding was rich in a similar fashion. He might not possess a title or an old, venerable family name, but he was plump in the pocket. Violet would soon know what it was like to have more than one house and servants waiting on her hand and foot in each of them.

"Are you still hungry?" he asked abruptly, standing from the bench and offering her his hand very correctly. She looked up from that broad palm he held open to her. He smiled down at her mildly, awaiting her response.

"Yes. Thank you." Now that her queasiness had passed, she realized she was famished. She had planned to find something to eat with Olympia. Indeed, she had forgotten all about that.

She rose to her feet and accepted his arm, frowning as her thoughts settled darkly on her missing friend. She felt a stab of guilt that she had forgotten all about her.

"There are several supper boxes near the front," he said as they set off.

He caught a glimpse of her face and paused. "What is it? Are you feeling ill again?" He glanced around as though looking for the ideal place for her to retch once more.

"No, no." She shook her head and inhaled deeply. "It's not that. It's Olympia. We haven't found her, and I'm a terrible person because—" She stopped suddenly.

She'd already been too open with him, too revealing. She was comfortable enough to be herself only ever around Olympia and, at times, Aster.

But with him, with Jacob, her walls seemed to crumble to dust. She couldn't imagine it would be that way with the eligible men her mother would inevitably push on her. There would never be this ease, this intimacy.

It was strange how familiar she felt with him, how close, and she had met him only today.

But why not? Why could she not have this?

She would never see him again.

This was the point of the night, after all—to live, to embrace fun, and to find adventure. And so far, Jacob had proved himself to be a gentleman.

"Because what?" he prompted her to finish.

"Because I'm enjoying myself," she admitted, releasing a nervous huff. "Dreadful animal-baiting aside, of course."

"Of course," he echoed.

"I'm enjoying myself when I *should* only be looking for Olympia." Heat climbed up her neck, igniting her face at this shameful admission. "I forgot my own dear friend, who is probably worried out of her head and actually looking for me." She gestured in agitation to the vastness of the Gardens. "Meanwhile, I'm here with you and having an unexpectedly delightful time and I'm an absolute wretch for it."

He stared at her for a long moment, his dark eyes contemplative. "You're not a wretch. You're human." He paused to shrug. "There is nothing wrong with enjoying yourself as you search. It's Vauxhall. A veritable garden of delights. How can you *unsee* what's happening around you? We'll find her. If she hasn't left for home, we will find her."

Prim shook her head miserably. It was getting late. She could only hazard a guess at the hour. "Have you any idea the time?" she asked abruptly.

"I, ah . . ." He fumbled inside his jacket and pulled out a pocket watch. "It's half past eleven."

"Half past eleven," she repeated, an edge of shrillness to her voice. The night was getting away from her. His company was distracting on multiple levels.

She swallowed and this time managed to speak in a much calmer voice. "It's half past eleven and I don't know where Olympia is."

She was nowhere to be seen. Prim's dearest friend was lost.

Perhaps scared or hurt or—

She silenced her thoughts, stopping them from going down that dark path.

"I'm a wretch," she mumbled again for good measure.

"Not true. You're a clever and sweet girl."

Her chest seized tightly. He thought her clever? And sweet? *And a girl* . . .

She inwardly cringed. That last bit stung. He didn't have to haul her from that tavern and then attach himself to her side, but he did so because he thought her a sweet girl. A *child* needing care.

He stayed with her to keep her safe. It was an obligatory compulsion because he was an honorable man. She was not so naïve as to believe chivalry was inherent among the gentry. Not every nob was so noble, but this one was—*he* was.

Jacob was helping her as she would have a child she found lost on the street. It was a necessary reminder, she supposed. She was not special to him. All the feelings she was experiencing were exclusive to her alone. There might be only a small age difference between them, but the gulf might as well have been the English Channel for as wide and yawning as it felt.

At ten and nine, Jacob was of great consequence. That much was evident. That was his birthright. Green as she might be, Prim was cognizant of the differences between them better than anyone. As the fourth-born daughter in a family of modest resources with a social-climbing mama, how could she not be aware?

She'd allowed herself an infatuation with him. It had started at Gunter's when he was simply a stranger with a handsome face, but now, over the last few hours, it had developed into something more. Something of substance. She didn't have much experience with . . . well, anything. But this felt special. It felt real.

Prim winced. She must stop that line of thinking so as not to suffer a bruised heart at the end of this night. She would never see him again. She knew that and she should not forget it.

Prim opened her mouth to respond, and then she froze. Speech was beyond her. She could only stare. No air passed her lips to fill her lungs. All of her was as still as stone, frozen as though that could somehow make her invisible.

Ironic, was it not? Wanting to be invisible when tonight had started as an exercise in being seen. Not reputation-ending visibility, of course. She had not wanted to be discovered. Simply *seen*. A participant in the world, not just an observer. She had wanted an adventure—a brief taste of freedom for one night.

Now all of that was about to come to an end.

Disaster headed her way.

~~The only thing a proper lady should do with her lips when in the company of a gentleman is smile demurely.~~

—*Lady Druthers's Guide to Perfect Deportment and Etiquette*

A gentleman who doesn't care to hear your thoughts isn't worth your time. You would be better served talking to yourself.

Chapter Ten

The disaster marching Prim's way was in the form of Redding. He and his friends were walking directly toward her. And she was without her mask. Exposed. One step—one glance—from ruin.

No no no no no.

Certainly standing as rigid as a statue wouldn't help her plight. She attempted to speak again, but no words came. Panic coated her tongue, acrid as smoke. She cast a desperate glance behind her to the bench where she'd retched so ignominiously earlier. Her domino lay on the ground beside it, sad and forlorn and out of her reach.

What had she been thinking in discarding it and then forgetting to put it back on? True, it likely had a little vomit on it, but she should have overlooked that for the sake of caution. Now she found herself in quite a predicament.

She touched her face—felt her skin smooth and bare for all the world to see—and knew fear.

Jacob looked down at her beside him, not taking note of the approaching group. "Is anything amiss?"

Move. Speak.

Prim's gaze never left the group of young bucks heading their way. One of Redding's friends elbowed him and nodded in their direction, evidently spotting them. Or rather, Jacob.

The group of young men slowed, but continued in their advance. They exchanged knowing glances as they inched closer up the path.

Closer to Primrose and Jacob.

"Primrose—"

She turned and clasped Jacob's arm, digging her fingers into him in a hope to silence him from saying her name again. His bicep felt surprisingly strong and wiry under her fingers. For a man leading an allegedly leisurely life, there was nothing soft about him. *Pull yourself together, Prim. Now is not the time to be thinking of his strong arms and how they might feel wrapped around you.*

Fortunately, her sudden movement silenced him from uttering her name aloud again. He looked down at her questioningly, arching a single eyebrow.

She was not entirely certain Redding even knew her given name. He'd never spoken it within her hearing, but they had been in each other's company on occasion. She'd always felt terribly uneasy under his regard—however infrequent it was. There was something in the way he looked at her, his gaze skimming over her from the top of her unfashionable red hair down to her slippered feet.

Or perhaps it was the way he *failed* to look at her—as though she were not even really present. As though she were as inconsequential as a gnat.

The gentlemen were still talking and exchanging glances as they moved forward, and it was indisputable. They knew Jacob—or at least one of them did—and they were approaching to speak to him.

Prim's gaze darted around as though an escape route would reveal itself.

Blood rushed in her ears, mixing with the pounding of her heart. She had to do something—preferably something that drew *less* attention to herself and not more.

They were coming, closing in like the four horsemen of the apocalypse.

However much an overstatement, the dark thought felt fitting. Once Redding took his eyes off Jacob long enough to get a good look at her, the jig would be up. He would recognize her—she was Violet's sister, after all—and she'd be finished. He would mention spotting Prim at Vauxhall to her mother and the consequences would be catastrophic. She could well imagine Mama's voice. In all likelihood, Prim would suffer permanent hearing loss from the volume of her scolding.

"Primrose?"

"Shhh!" She waved a hand desperately over her lips, her heart giving a pained little squeeze at the sound of her name.

Jacob followed her panicked gaze to the group of men. "Do you know one of—"

"I must go." She shook her head. "I cannot be seen. *He* cannot see me." Without another word, she fled with a gulp of breath in a graceless dash.

Thankfully, he did not call out to her again.

Without a doubt she was attracting notice running away as she was, but it was just the back of her. She must get herself out of sight. She dared not look over her shoulder, lest Redding glimpse her face. Her heart pounded hard with the fear of discovery.

If Mama found out . . .

Prim could not imagine what her mother would do precisely, but she could well imagine her display of temper. Mama could be loud and fierce. Prim had witnessed her scream at Papa until her face turned nine shades of red. Prim dove onto a narrower path, determined to avoid that scenario at all costs. There would be no red-mottled-faced tantrums from her mother. Not if Prim could help it.

The narrow path was deserted. Trees and hedges encroached, pressing in on the row from all sides like watchful sentries. The sudden and absolute isolation felt unnatural. To find such a dark and lonely place, separated from the rest of the lively Gardens was abnormal . . . and deliberate. This place clearly existed for its very seclusion.

She was glad for the lack of people, but where had everyone gone?

Then it dawned on her.

She was on an infamous dark walk. Where couples took

sanctuary for clandestine activities. The very place she had been warned to avoid by that lady she shared a boat with earlier in the evening. And by Lady Kettering.

Prim stalled for a moment and glanced over her shoulders before squaring them and continuing on cautiously.

There was no help for it.

If she turned back around and was discovered . . .

She shook her head. The threat of being recognized was the greater peril—far more ominous—than continuing forward.

Onward she would go. She thought she heard voices and footsteps somewhere behind her, and so she hastened her strides. Perhaps it was a manifestation of her overwrought nerves or the consequence of reading too many gothic novels, but at the snap of a twig, she lifted her skirts and ran.

Rushing blindly along the path, Prim shuddered in the warm summer night as though a wintry wind were scuttling over her. If Redding identified her, if she were caught, Mama would postpone her coming out. Her mother had promised she had to wait only until Aster became betrothed, but she could make it longer. She *would* make it longer.

Prim could be twenty before she entered Society. Or older. Or not make a debut at all. Mama held all the power. If she caught wind of Prim's antics tonight, she could decide to keep Primrose at home to be her permanent spinster daughter, tasked with caring for her and Papa as they slid into their dotage. It happened in families with multiple children often enough. Prim, however, never imagined spending her life in the role of caregiver to her parents. She could not fight back a wince at that prospect.

Emboldened by the resolve these thoughts inspired, she lifted her skirts higher in both hands so that her strides could be longer, quicker. Her shoes flew over the cobbles. Deep male voices—possibly Redding and his friends—drifted from somewhere in the distance behind her, and she knew they were not imaginary.

Prim sucked in a panicked mouthful of air and swung a left when the path bisected. Soon the row presented several options. Left, right, straight. She was caught in a maze. She stopped and pressed back against a hedge to catch her breath and listen for voices and to see if they were in pursuit of her. Gulping down the excess saliva in her mouth, she held still and listened.

There was only silence.

Snap.

No imagining *that.*

She jerked her head to the side, listening intently and peering into the darkness in the direction of the sound. The moon overhead offered a little illumination. She could at least identify the parameters of the dark row and that no other figures appeared to lurk anywhere. Then she looked to her other side.

She was well and truly alone. She'd escaped Redding.

But she had also lost Jacob. Her heart sank. Losing Olympia was bad enough. Now she'd lost him, too.

As she peered into the fathomless night, she brushed her palms back and forth against the prickly leaves of the hedge behind her.

She was alone now and on one of the dark walks she had intended to avoid. She could hear the voice of the lady from the boat even now, warning her not to stray onto a dark walk, and her own promising she would not. At the time she had meant it.

And yet here she was with her heart in her throat. Alone on a dark walk.

She was not certain how next to proceed.

Prim observed how the hedges encroaching on each side of the row seemed to be a veritable black swath. The path itself was murky as smoke, but the shrubberies were even darker. They felt ominous—pulsing, living walls of vegetation hemming her in but also hiding the unknown.

She had never felt so vulnerable in her life. Alone and yet aware that anyone could be about—a fact that was especially emphasized when the shrubbery rustled nearby. It shook for just for a moment, and then it stopped. It couldn't be a squirrel. As far as she knew they were not nocturnal.

Prim pressed a hand flat over her breast, as though she could keep her pounding heart from exploding free. She stepped back from the hedge to the center of the path. It was as far as she could get from the wall of shrubs where something hid. She then rotated in a small circle, trying to determine the origin of the sound.

It started again. Somewhere to her right. She swung that way, staring into the dark hedge full of shaking leaves as if she could see through the dense foliage.

A low moan rose up to accompany the whispering leaves. She cocked her head, straining to listen. The moan was decidedly female, and then the sound twisted into sharp anguish.

Prim stepped forward. "Hello. Are you hurt?" she called.

The moaning continued, either indifferent or unaware of

her. Then another voice joined the cacophony. This one clearly male. He cried out gutturally.

The two sounds merged in violent accord. One shrill, the other rough as grit.

Suddenly it dawned on Prim. No one was hurt. On the contrary, someone—*someones*—were very much the opposite of hurt.

Buried in the shrubbery, a pair of lovers was in the midst of an assignation. *Of course.* That was what people did in the dark rows of Vauxhall, after all.

Heat scored her face. She didn't feel quite threatened anymore—no creature or villain was going to pounce out and tackle her, but she was scandalized to learn that she was mere feet away from people in the throes of congress. She had not thought herself easily scandalized. Apparently, she was more callow than she'd realized.

She had thought that listening to all of Olympia's stories of her experiences in London—and even before then, in Germany—to say nothing of all of Prim's extensive and incessant reading, had prepared her for instances of brazenness. It wasn't as though she were the one up to naughty antics in the shrubs.

Her head whipped left and right again, searching. She needed to find her way out of here at once.

Turning to flee, she collided smack into another individual. She had not noticed his approach amid her focus on the couple in the hedge. The force of the collision snapped her head back.

Hard hands came up to seize her arms. "Och! Oy, easy now! Wot we 'ave 'ere?"

"Looks like a dove lost 'er way." This came from a second man.

Her stomach sank. Not just one man but two. She pulled back, stepping clear of the figures to peer at them.

They were of her age. Shabbily attired. And . . . perhaps familiar.

"Strayed off the path, 'ave ye? Need 'elp finding yer way back?" The one speaking was in possession of a top hat with an exceedingly wide brim.

The hat was memorable, as was the wild nest of curls that sprang out around the wide brim.

These were the same footpads who had accosted Jacob earlier! The same ones *she* drove away. Fortunately, they did not seem to recognize her as the person who had threatened to call the Watch on them.

Top Hat elbowed his companion. "Lost yer way down a dark walk?" He tsked. "No' a very good idea."

At that particular moment, the couple trysting in the bushes reached epic proportions on the scale of sound. Truly, it was decibel shattering.

Top Hat's friend chuckled. "Sounds like they're 'aving a bit o' fun in there, Simon."

"Right so," Simon agreed. "Why don't ye go relieve them of their purses?"

Simon settled his gleaming gaze on her. "And we'll relieve ye of yer reticule as well, miss, and anything else of value ye might 'ave."

His words reverberated ominously in the air as she touched the reticule dangling from her wrist, testing its weight slightly, wishing it had the heft of a brick so that she might strike him.

The other footpad must have found his quarry in the undergrowth. There was a masculine curse and the woman let loose a scream that did not originate in passion, unlike her earlier sounds. Simon released a snort of laughter and looked in their direction, a disturbing grin on his face.

Primrose quaked, feeling ill at the sight of that grin and all it signified. He was enjoying the distress he inflicted. He was not some fairy-tale Robin Hood, thieving only to support himself and his family. He enjoyed what he did like the true villain he was. These were wicked men, and she could not trust them *not* to harm her. She could not trust that they would take her purse and release her safely.

"You there, Simon, my dear lad!" A woman's voice cracked over the air and shot a bolt of relief through Prim. Her shoulders sagged a bit as the tension escaped and she peered around Simon, searching for this sudden ally. Certainly this woman would put a stop to this nefarious activity. She was easy to mark even on the murky path. She strolled their way, her hips rolling in a mesmeric sashay, the skirts of her bold orange dress swishing in the air. The gown was outdated, the skirts too full, more in fashion with the gowns her mother wore as a girl. It showed a great deal of wear and was soiled in spots.

"Good even', Nell." Simon touched his hat circumspectly in a strange display of manners.

Nell slapped a hand against the side of her skirts. "Find a pigeon, did ye? Why don't ye be a fine lad and share the reward with an ol' friend, eh?"

Prim gaped for a moment as the two spoke, indifferent to her presence.

Simon scoffed. "When 'ave ye ever shared yer loot with me?"

She tsked. "Don't be greedy, Simon."

Clearly Primrose had miscalculated. She was a little ashamed of her assumption in light of the reality of the situation. Of course a woman could be the villain, too. She had read enough Shakespeare to know that. She should not have assumed so suddenly that the fairer sex could commit no wrongdoing. It was naïve of her.

More and more tonight, she was learning that she was naïve in many ways. She had craved this, the outside world, but it wasn't all fun and adventure.

"I don't even know what she 'as in 'er purse yet."

Nell shifted her attention to Prim, looking her over with an assessing eye. "Nice gown."

Prim's hand flew to her bodice. "Th-thank you." No sense explaining how it was not her gown but one she had borrowed.

Nell reached out to touch her sleeve, stroking the fabric in admiration. "Very nice. Take it off. I'll be keeping it."

~~Women are delicate creatures that must be cosseted.~~

—Lady Druthers's Guide to
Perfect Deportment and Etiquette

Childbirth.

Chapter Eleven

Primrose must have misunderstood the woman. Why would she want her gown? She gave her head a little shake as though that might help clear it.

"The gown," Nell repeated. "Remove it."

"Begging your pardon?" Prim asked, tugging her arm away and taking a step back. Surely Nell would not strip the dress off her back. That could not be her intention.

Simon chuckled. "What ye going to do with 'er dress, Nell?"

Nell squared her shoulders. "Why wear it, of course. I'll look quite the lady, don't you think?"

Simon jerked a thumb in Prim's direction. "This one's got more meat on 'er than ye. It won't even fit. The thing will hang off ye."

Nell slapped his arm. "Watch yer tongue. I'll not 'ave ye insulting another woman for the shape the good Lord saw fit to bless 'er with."

Simon sputtered, gesturing at Primrose. "I merely pointed out that ye and she do not—"

"Enough." Nell waved a finger to silence him. "Next thing you'll be insulting me."

Prim looked back and forth between them in bewilderment. One moment she was being deprived of her reticule—and quite possibly her dress—and in the next a lady thief was jumping to her defense.

All hope that the theft of her gown was forgotten fled when Nell looked back at her and directed, "Your dress, please, miss." The fact that she was smiling as she uttered the polite request did nothing to ease its sting.

"You'll leave me . . . naked?" *Certainly not.*

Nell shook her head with a tsk. "I'm not that heartless. Of course I would not subject ye to that indignity. I'll leave ye in yer shift and chemise and petticoats. Ye can find yer way to the main path and some gentleman will certainly be gallant enough to provide ye with his jacket."

She made it sound so very reasonable. As though a woman being relieved of her gown in public would be neither traumatic nor reputation ruining. Prim made no move to undress, of course. How could she?

"I don't think she 'eard ye," Simon offered.

Nell sent him an irritated glance, and Primrose took her chance and swung her reticule, hoping the weight of the coins she carried would be enough to inflict some pain.

Her blow knocked Simon's top hat off his head. "Oww!" Simon staggered, clutching his bared head as the hat toppled to the ground.

Nell released a short cry and reached out to grasp his arm.

Prim did not wait to take measure of the extent of her damage. She knew she could not have inflicted much. She only hoped it would give her enough time to escape.

Turning, she fled down the path, her feet pounding over the cobbles, trying to get as far as possible before they could give pursuit. Perhaps they wouldn't. Perhaps they would decide she wasn't worth the trouble.

She was mistaken again. That had been happening a lot tonight.

Shouts chased after her, and she risked a look behind her before she turned down onto another row. Nell, Simon, and the other man were giving chase.

Splendid. Apparently, the bandit in the shrubs had resurfaced. All three were fleet of foot, as only veteran cutpurses could be. She had long since lost track of direction. Prim didn't know if she was close to exiting onto a well-lit row or diving deeper into Vauxhall's dark labyrinth of walks.

She couldn't stop to assess. There was no time. She was most certain, however, that Nell and her friends knew their way exceedingly well through this maze of paths.

Prim swung a right and ran directly into a tall figure.

"Oof!" she cried out, jarred from the impact.

Firm hands came up to her arms, steadying her. She lifted her gaze and the fight went out of her. She almost crumpled against him. Happy tears pricked her eyes.

"Primrose," Jacob breathed, relief crossing his face. She felt that same sentiment in equal measure, perhaps more, echoing through her.

Simon shouted in the distance behind them. "Where did she go?"

Primrose jerked at the sound—the voice like a physical jab.

Jacob looked over her head. "Who—"

"The footpads. The same two from earlier and a woman."

"Bloody hell." He seized her hand and looked around wildly for a moment.

Before she realized his intent, he pulled her after him into the shrubbery.

"Crawl," he instructed in hushed tones as he dropped down on his knees, clearing the way before them with his bigger body, shoving with bare hands at the leaves springing in their path.

She did as he instructed and scurried after him, no doubt dirtying her beautiful borrowed gown and snagging the fine fabric. She winced, hoping it was not ruined, and then she had to bite back the ridiculous urge to laugh. If it *was* ruined, would Nell still want it? Whatever the case, a soiled gown was better than no gown at all. Olympia would agree with that.

The branches and leaves loosened up around them, allowing him to turn to face the path. She followed and settled down on her belly beside him.

Propped on their elbows, they stared through the cracks and openings of the branches. The loamy musk of earth filled her nose.

The footpads rounded the corner and stopped.

"She turned this way! I saw 'er, I did!" the familiar voice of Simon insisted.

"Perhaps' she dove into the 'edge," Nell supplied.

Prim's heart jumped in her chest and she gave a small gasp at Nell's unerring guess. The sound escaped louder than she'd intended, and Jacob's hand quickly covered her mouth.

Her gaze shot to his face, to his dark eyes so close and shining in warning. Their noses almost bumped as they listened to the ruffians a few yards away.

Together, they turned and looked back out at the walk again, watching as one pair of boots, presumably Simon's, turned to face the hedge where they hid.

"Ye' want to go up and down, tearing through this long line of shrub looking for 'er when we could be 'unting other nobs?" the second footpad demanded.

"She smacked me in the 'ead," Simon grumbled. "Dented my 'at. Seems only right that I teach the little witch a lesson."

Prim flinched and Jacob's other hand came up to her shoulder, giving it a comforting squeeze.

"She's gone," Nell stated, her voice flatly reasonable.

"Very well. Did ye' at least finish with the couple tupping in the bushes?"

"Aye, I collected their purses."

"Good then. Let us go. There be plenty of other quarry about tonight." There was a low rumble of conversation as their feet started away.

Primrose waited, listening to the sound of their footsteps fading into the distance. She and Jacob remained where they were, cushioned on the soft earth, buried among the leaves, inhaling the pungent earthy air.

The sound of her breaths filled her ears. Jacob's hand still covered her mouth. Her lips pressed to his palm, as intimate as

a kiss, and she felt suddenly, horribly self-conscious, achingly aware of his closeness.

Their proximity alone was a scandal. Everything about this moment . . . about the two of them buried in a hedge on a dark walk, was a perfect scandal and would ruin Prim's reputation should it ever come to light.

A bubble of laughter welled up in her chest. She giggled against his hand. She could not help it. It was the height of absurdity. She was hiding in the bushes with a nob. She had lost her best friend in a tavern brawl, been accosted by footpads, *and* now she was rolling around on the ground with a blueblood, soiling her gown. Giggles were hard to fight.

She doubted he had ever sullied himself in such a manner before. At least not since he was a lad in leading strings, his nurse trying unsuccessfully to keep him from falling to the ground.

His eyes widened at her muffled giggles and then he laughed, too—a low, deep chuckle that turned her skin to gooseflesh. His hand softened against her lips, as though he'd remembered he still held it there covering her mouth. He lifted it away and she swung her head around to fully look at him.

"I think they've gone," she whispered with a tremulous smile.

"So they have," he returned, smiling back at her.

His features were but vague shadow—the line of his jaw and nose, his deep-set eyes. The flash of white teeth as his lips moved.

"Should we linger a moment to be certain?" she suggested. "In case it is a trap, and they are waiting for us emerge?"

"A sound notion," he replied, those shadow lips moving, sending puffs of air toward her mouth.

It was overwhelming.

Her body felt aflame, her senses overwrought. Another moment alone with him like this, and she might combust. And yet she had made the recommendation that they remain. Clearly Prim had lost her head. But at least she hadn't lost her gown.

His hand lifted back toward her and she gave a small gasp, pulling back.

"May I?" he asked.

He paused, holding his hand midair, and she felt foolish.

She wasn't certain what he wanted, but she gave a nod of assent.

After a moment, his hand continued, landing in her hair, working through tangled strands. Her elegant arrangement was not so elegant anymore. Most of her hair had tumbled free, the pins scattered and lost.

"Here," he murmured as he tugged something loose. When he withdrew his hand, she saw that he held a spiny leaf between his fingers. "You had a bit of bramble in your hair."

"Thank you," she said softly. She tore her gaze from him to face the path again, but it did no good. She could feel his stare on the side of her face leaving a wake of heat where it roamed, as palpable as touch.

How long must they wait?

Expelling a deep breath, she faced him again. She locked eyes with a gaze of dark glowing embers.

"How did you find me?" she asked. "After I left you, how did you . . ."

"You mean after you ran like the dogs of hell were after you?"

She winced and gave a light laugh. "Yes. After that."

"A Higher Power must have led me to you."

She smiled in the darkness. "That's a bit of whimsy. I didn't know you had such a fanciful streak in you, my lord."

"I've a great many depths . . . and I thought you weren't going to call me that anymore." The air from his words, the movement of his mouth, whispered against her lips.

"No one can hear us here," she replied, and it was best, safer, to resort to formality. Especially here in this most-intimate situation.

"*I* can hear you. And I like the sound of my name on your lips."

"Oh." She breathed the word more than spoke it.

Tension hummed in the air and she wondered if he felt it too. Or was it just Prim?

She was all awkwardness, huddled on the ground with him. Even in the reduced light, he seemed steady and confident in a way only a man in full control of his world could be.

"You must not say things like that."

"Why not?"

She mulled that over. Indeed. *Why not?*

Because his words, his voice, twisted her up inside.

Because words like that made her feel overly warm. They made her like him more than she should. They made her forget the world she belonged to and the world that awaited her.

Rather than answer him with any of those things though, she cleared her throat. "Do you think we should—"

His head dipped and he kissed her, pressing his mouth over hers.

Never had Prim imagined a kiss taking place outside the bounds of a betrothal. That had been one of the many tenets she'd memorized from the rigid Lady Druthers's book. Intimacy between a man and woman prior to the posting of the marriage banns was simply not done. *Forbidden.* The public announcement of a couple's forthcoming nuptials had to be made before a kiss was ever exchanged.

In truth, Mrs. Druthers warned against such intimacy *before* the exchange of marriage vows. Aster had told Prim that she had caught Violet and Redding in a heated embrace, sharing a kiss. Prim found that surprising, as Violet, who courted Mama's favor in all situations, often parroted the tenets from Lady Druthers's book, and succeeded in making Prim and Aster look absolutely inept.

In any event, Prim had not thought she would want to kiss someone after only a day, but she wanted this with every pore, every quivering fiber of her person. His mouth on hers was real and true and she wouldn't change it, for all of the trouble she had found herself in tonight.

It was a strange set of circumstances that had even brought her here, to this moment with him. She would not have another opportunity like it again. It would be just this once.

She'd already vowed there would be only this one night of adventure. One night in which she had to make every moment count. A moment to be a little more Prim, and a little less proper.

The kiss was as fleeting as it was sudden. He eased back, his breath fanning her lips.

His dark eyes darted over her face, touching everywhere.

"Have I offended?" His voice husked over her lips.

"No," she replied shakily, her tongue darting out to wet her lips. "I . . . I have no objection if you want to do that again."

"Oh I want to do it again. Very much."

~~Some may say it's permissible to kiss a gentleman~~ ~~to whom one is engaged, but I urge young ladies~~ ~~to say *no!* to this, *no, no*. A lady's virtue must be~~ ~~maintained at all times.~~

—*Lady Druthers's Guide to Perfect Deportment and Etiquette*

A lady should decide where her lips go.

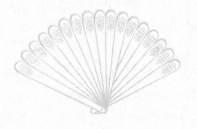

Chapter Twelve

*S*he closed the space this time—which really wasn't any distance at all, considering they had perfected the art of talking against each other's lips.

This kiss was different.

Less tentative.

Prim started it, angling her mouth against his, reveling in the increasing pressure.

Jacob's hand settled on her shoulder, grasping, molding to the curved shape before sliding down around her back and hauling her in until their bodies were fully meshed. Lying on her side, she could feel the beat of his heart through his clothing as it thumped against her breast.

The kiss grew between them. Deepened until she knew the shape and texture and taste of him. Until it became a thing that was its own life—a force that pulsed and turned and altered.

Just as she thought she knew what this kiss was, it became something else. Something hotter. Something that made her knees tremble. Something that sent sensations to places she had largely ignored all her life. Parts of her body she had never thought of other than in a functional way.

She parted her lips and his tongue licked inside her mouth, making contact with her own. She jerked, startled, and pulled back.

He pressed his forehead to hers, his breath falling ragged. "Apologies. I did not—"

"Is that . . . done? People do that?"

"With tongues?" he queried. "Yes, when they like each other well enough and want to."

He liked her enough. He wanted to? "And you want to . . . with me?"

It was incomprehensible that the gentleman from Gunter's this morning—that dashing, handsome, confident gentleman—could now desire her in this way.

"I want what brings you pleasure. Only that."

She shuddered, certain that no one, other than herself, had ever put her pleasure first. There were too many things, too many *others,* too many blasted *sisters* who came before her.

She moistened her lips and kissed him again. An open-mouthed kiss, her tongue tentative, tasting his bottom lip, and she understood.

She understood want and desire and what poets had been talking about when they waxed on using grandiose metaphors.

He kissed her back, deeper, his tongue caressing, stroking, and oh . . . she *understood.*

His hand moved to her face, cupping her cheek, fingers delving into her hair as their lips tasted each other.

The fresh scent of earth rose around them as they rolled on the ground, leaves rustling about them, snagging at her hair, but she did not care.

The kissing went on and on, but still, it was not enough.

Eternity would not be enough.

Heads slanted, turning at different angles for a deeper taste, but it never seemed enough.

His hand was on her face, her shoulder, then her back, then her hair again.

Jacob's heart found its rhythm, matching the beat of hers.

Prim wasn't certain who stopped first. Or how they came apart. Or how long they'd been locked together.

A long time.

It *had* to have been a long time. A lifetime had passed during the span of that kiss.

Their breathing mingled in heavy pants, noses aligned and touching.

She clutched the lapels of his jacket, holding on to him tightly, fingers flexing in fabric, unable and unwilling to let go.

"That was . . ." Her voice faded on a gulp. "I wish it weren't so dark. I wish I could see your face." The better to remember this moment.

She inhaled, imprinting his scent on her mind—that faint whiff of cologne and soap and summer—adding it to the dark corners, another layer in the memory she would keep forever of this night.

"You know my face," he whispered. "I see yours. In my mind, I see you." His finger stroked down the bridge of her nose. "Those freckles you have. The fine arch of your eyebrows, a shade darker than your brilliant hair."

He kissed her again, lighter, savoring before he lifted up. She chased after his mouth with a small whimper.

"We should go," he murmured.

Of course.

They couldn't remain buried in a hedge on a dark walk forever. Their little bubble would not keep. It had to be burst. And it had to be past midnight by now. She was afraid to ask for verification of that. "Very well."

They crawled out of the hedge. Leaving was more difficult than entering. They'd been all haste then, fear driving them. Now the leaves and branches seemed to grab at them, snatching and pulling at her as though unwilling to relinquish her back to the world.

She emerged with an exerted breath. He helped her to her feet. They dusted at their garments. She touched her hair, wincing at the mess of it.

"Here. I went back for it." He held out her domino to her.

"That was thoughtful. Thank you. I suppose I must." She tied it back on, feeling a little deflated in the process. For however little protection it provided, she was once again returning to masks. To hiding. Soon that would be her whole life—hiding from her true hopes and desires.

He held out his hand for her to take. No arm. They were past that formality, and her heart flipped over inside her chest.

She slid her hand into his, her heart now squeezing at the sensation of his warm fingers wrapping around hers. It felt good. "Now, let's go find your friend."

Her earlier moment of deflation took an even deeper plunge, sinking into unaccountable disappointment.

Find her friend, of course. That thing she should have been doing all along.

They would find Olympia, and then they would put this night behind them. She would say farewell to him.

She might have become hopelessly turned around within the network of shadowed paths, but he seemed to know directly how to proceed.

"You're quite adept at maneuvering the dark walks," she remarked.

He looked down at her and his dark eyes glinted with light. "I've always had a wonderful sense of direction."

She snorted. "I'm sure of that."

He'd likely been here before. A face like his would attract any number of pretty young ladies ready to cast aside propriety.

He escorted her with purpose toward the nearest exit.

"What happened to those men?" she asked as she contemplated that they would soon step back out onto the well-lighted row. Surely Redding had moved on by now. "The group of men that was approaching us when I ran away?"

"Oh. One of them knew me from my club. Or rather he believed he knew me. We once sat at the same card table." He shrugged. "I didn't recall him."

"I imagine that happens often. People approaching you on some pretext or another."

He angled his head. "I suppose—"

She laughed. "Goodness. You don't even know, do you?"

"Know what?"

"How very sought after you are."

"Sought after?"

"Indeed. At Gunter's, and here . . . people gawk at you. They approach you like excitable puppies." He could not be so oblivious. Or perhaps that was the blessing and curse of such privilege? A complete unawareness of your own good fortune. That was the nature of it, she supposed. "How many invitations do you receive? Daily?"

He shrugged. "I don't know. My secretary leaves them on my desk. Sometimes I browse them."

She shook her head. "*Sometimes.* You're a marvel. I'm going to assume the majority of those invitations come from mothers with marriageable daughters longing for you to attend their parties."

"Yes. And you know why they want me, don't you?" He shuddered. "I can't even contemplate marriage. Not for some years yet."

She laughed. "Years? That's rich. If only all those mamas knew that was your plan."

She sobered. *Some* years from now would see her married to someone vetted by her parents. She'd likely be a mother. She'd be fully enmeshed in a life her husband fashioned and controlled whilst Jacob was still a wealthy bachelor living solely for himself.

The dichotomy shouldn't have angered her.

But it did.

Her sisters never questioned their roles. Aster might not have liked it, and did little to hide her aversion, but she did not protest beyond rolled eyes and well-timed sighs. They simply accepted their lives and made the best of them. Went blithely and biddably along with Mama's plans and Lady Druthers's rules.

Prim was here in defiance of that docile acceptance. Tonight was about Prim doing something for herself, celebrating her birthday when no one else would, but it was also about resistance to this world she was born into, even if she had no choice but to return to it before dawn streaked the sky.

"Why do you frown?" he asked.

"I'm thinking how fortunate you are."

"And that makes you frown," he teased.

"You're fortunate and don't even know it."

"What do you mean?"

"You can go where you want. Do what you want. You have choice. Independence. You don't have to marry . . . at all, ever, if that is your wish."

He said nothing. His lips pressed into a flat line, for he could not disagree. He knew she was right.

"Such are the vagaries of fate," she continued. "Had I been born male to a wealthy family . . ." Her voice faded.

"Then you'd be me," he finished for her.

"Indeed. I would be you. I would be free."

"But you're not free now," he murmured, as though turning that over, contemplating it, letting it roll within the pleats of his mind. There was a difference, she realized, between knowing and *knowing*.

A quick glance at his face revealed his own deepening frown. Apparently, he did not like the thought of that.

That made two of them.

They approached the end of the dark walk. The well-lit main row loomed ahead. He paused and turned to face her. His hands came up to rest on her shoulders.

"What are you . . ."

He reached out and curled his fingers around the back of her neck, underneath the heavy weight of her hair. The sensation of his warm fingers on her nape sent a jolt through her.

"Once more." His gaze fell on her mouth. "Before we rejoin the world?"

"Oh," she sighed, her nerves catching fire again.

He pulled her against him, pressing his body into hers.

Sensation flooded her. He plucked another twig from her hair and tossed it aside. That barest brush of his fingers in her hair made her skin tighten.

He was so much larger than Prim. She could feel him — the lean lines of him, the flat plane of his chest and stomach against her.

Their noses almost touched as their breaths mingled.

His brown eyes glowed darkly, traveling over her face until they landed on her mouth. For a few moments he held still, staring at her lips. As though he was giving her a chance, the choice to stop this from happening.

His hand flexed on the back of her neck, the pads of his fingers branding points of heat.

Her heart hammered like a trapped bird inside her chest.

"Very well," she agreed, giving her permission as though he

were waiting for it. And perhaps he was, because the moment she uttered the words, his mouth claimed hers.

His lips slanted over hers hotly, and she was back in that hedge with him. Their lips reunited. His teeth gently tugged on her bottom lip and her belly coiled tightly. His fingers burrowed into her hair, caressing her scalp and shooting tingles down her spine. He released her bottom lip and gave it a long, savoring lick before diving back into the kiss.

Prim's knees wobbled and she grabbed and held fast to his jacket to keep from falling. It was brash and bold, but she didn't care. All she cared about was him. About the taste of his lips, about his strong body fused to her. His warm, sweet tongue in her mouth, exploring and tasting and making her want to crawl inside him.

This night, with him, was the best birthday gift she could have asked for.

With one hand still in her hair, he slid the other down her back, cupping her derrière through the fabric of her gown. He squeezed, pleasure rushing straight from his hand to all her secret places. She gasped into his mouth, her feet lifting up to her tiptoes.

"Ho, there!" a strange voice called out. "We can see you."

She gasped and pulled away, looking around, feeling dazed and unable to focus.

A voice called, "Find a room!" with a giggle.

Heat slashed Prim's face. Her eyes lit on a small party strolling past them on the main row, waving and laughing in their direction.

"Ah, Jacob?" She glanced back at him. "Should we—"

He dragged her back and resumed kissing her again. In full view.

She felt afire. Engulfed in flames.

It was swift and overwhelming in the best sense. She felt like she was drowning. They kissed for several more moments before she wedged a hand between them and broke the kiss.

Panting, he gazed down at her, his eyes gleaming in the dark.

Breathing raggedly, she reached for his face and touched his cheek, relishing in the texture, the faint scratch of bristles.

Prim felt his stare on her face, his warm breath on the side of her face.

Jacob's fingers wrapped around hers, clasping her hand against his face. He turned, pressing a kiss into the curve of her palm, and she felt the inexplicable and inappropriate urge to cry.

She blinked burning eyes and inhaled through her nose, reaching desperately for her fleeing composure. He finished his kiss and she pulled her hand away.

"Shall we go?" she queried.

He nodded and they stepped out together on the path.

~~A lady should never eat with gusto in front of a gentleman, lest she appear to be ruled by coarse needs.~~

—*Lady Druthers's Guide to Perfect Deportment and Etiquette*

Don't serve the good lemon tea cakes if you don't wish people to eat them.

Chapter Thirteen

The crowds had thinned somewhat on the main row. It felt different now than when she had first arrived at the start of the night with Olympia.

It was the same path dotted with glowing lamps, but less crowded. Less crowded, yes, but no less rowdy. The faint of heart had departed home for their beds. It had to be well after midnight. Only the boldest remained, ringing in the late hour.

Still, no glimpse of canary yellow. No Olympia.

"You did not finish explaining to me why you ran into the dark walk."

"I ran because—"

"You knew one of the men in the group," he finished.

"Yes." She nodded.

"I surmised as much. Who was he? A family acquaintance?"

"Ah. You could say that." She sighed. "Mr. Redding is betrothed to my sister. Violet is to wed him in a fortnight. Mama insists he's a catch. As much as Mama disapproves of those who work in trade, his family owns one of the largest mills in southern England. His pockets run deep. Money . . . opens all doors, no?" She winced. "Forgive me. I know it's gauche to speak of finances."

"I think we are well past worrying over what can and cannot be said to each other."

She stared at him and smiled slowly. He was right, of course.

Olympia was the only person in her life to whom she spoke with such candor. It felt good to have another person with whom she could converse in such a fashion.

"It's not that he is in trade that I find so distasteful." It was not even that he lacked intelligence. She felt wrong judging him for that. She was not the one marrying him, after all. If it didn't bother Violet that he was a lackwit, then why should it bother Prim? It was not even that he overindulged in drink. "It's how his family makes their money. They should pay their laborers a healthy wage." She could not help injecting a fair amount of censure into her voice.

"I take it your family does not share your disapproval?"

"Violet has agreed to marry him. She chose him over several other suitors. She is especially fond of the pretty things she shall have once they are wed. Mama is already planning trips to Bath, where he keeps a second home. The mills are little better than workhouses and I've told them as much. It's the height of irony that the same people who petition for the abolition of slavery also operate these mills."

"You're a bit of a reformer, Primrose." Admiration tinged his voice. "Too bad you don't have a seat in Parliament."

"Indeed." It was a heady thought, to consider the change she could bring about if she were to hold such a position. She considered him a moment, realizing that Jacob was a person who could make real change happen. A man of wealth and, presumably, rank. He could bring about reform if he so chose.

He chuckled. "I have no doubt that in time you shall influence your future brother-in-law to do better. He's marrying your sister. Certainly you can influence her and she, in turn, can speak to her husband about improving conditions in his family's mill."

She snorted, even as she felt a flicker of hope that he was correct. "That is kind, but your faith in me is too great."

He studied her as they passed beneath the lights. "Don't underestimate yourself. I don't."

An awkward, tense moment fell. She didn't know what to say precisely to that compliment. He certainly knew how to make her feel good about herself.

She looked down, watching her slippered feet peeking out from beneath the hem of her gown as they strolled.

"There are several rallies and assemblies on such issues. You should attend. There are always a few ladies interested in social order and politics as you are. You would not be the only one present."

"Perhaps someday." When she was out from under her mother's thumb. She would like that very much.

"A girl who can sneak off to Vauxhall could certainly sneak away to an assembly."

"Would I gain very many stares with my mask?" She touched her domino with a smile.

His eyes roamed over her face. "I doubt it would be the domino to capture their attention," he murmured in a husky voice that made shivers break out on her skin.

Heat rose up her neck to her face. He was flirting. She did not know how to flirt. Instead, she lightly touched her loose coiffure. "Is it the hair?" The red could serve as a beacon.

He gave a short laugh. "That's its own enticement."

Heat flamed her face.

"Do you smell that?" Jacob lifted his nose in the air. "Food! Ambrosia."

She was so hungry anything would smell like ambrosia right now. The lemon biscuit (though delicious!) had hardly satisfied her. Now that her fear and excitement were waning, her stomach was cramping with hunger.

Still holding her hand, he led her toward a structure that resembled a theater house. It was Grecian in style, with cream-colored columns marking the front. Perhaps they performed plays inside.

They stopped before the façade. He held his arms wide. "Now this place will serve a fine meal."

"What is it?"

"A theater . . . of sorts."

The "of sorts" combined with the glint in his eyes told her it was definitely something more than a theater. But she trusted him. After all they had been through tonight, she knew he would never put her in an unfavorable situation. Rather it was she who had put Jacob in a few unfavorable situations . . .

He moved toward the front door and opened it, gesturing for her to enter.

Holding up her skirts, she swept inside, hoping for all the world that she did not look like someone who had just spent time rolling around in the dirt in a lovers' tryst.

Jacob passed some coin into an attendant's hand and they were led to a supper box. Jacob held out a chair for her and they were soon seated with a very elegantly arranged table between them, sipping champagne as an orchestra was revved up for the show.

She had not yet learned what manner of entertainment was to be provided. Whatever it was, it appeared to be on the verge of commencing. The promise of food, finally, at this very late hour, would have her endure almost anything.

"And what other kind of things did you plan on doing in your evening of adventure?" Jacob asked as he unfolded his napkin across his lap.

"Well." She reflected for a moment. "I wanted to drink spirits." Beyond the ratafia she had enjoyed. She lifted her champagne glass in salute.

"Done," he replied. "What else?"

"Well, I wanted to waltz." She fiddled with the napkin in her lap. It felt rather embarrassing to confess, but she wanted to dance beyond the dancing she practiced with her sisters in their parlor. "Since I haven't come out in Society and who knows when I will, I wanted to waltz."

"Waltz?"

She nodded, an embarrassing warmth creeping up her face. It probably seemed a very silly and inconsequential thing to him. "Yes."

"Well, we can rectify that."

"You don't have to—"

"Nonsense. There's dancing all about this Garden. We shall see to it after our meal."

A tremor of excitement fluttered through her. She would waltz with him.

"What else?" he prompted.

She reflected a bit more. "Oh, yes! Smoke a cigar."

"Smoke a cigar?" He blinked and waited a moment before chuckling.

"Papa and all his gentlemen friends smoke them in his study." She shrugged. "For once, I want to see what all the fuss is about."

"I think I can oblige you with this request."

He rose from the table and departed their box, approaching one of the hovering servers. In moments he was back, brandishing a cigar. He leaned forward to the small candle on the table, bringing the cigar to his lips, puffing on it until the end glowed.

"There you are." He held it out to her.

"Thank you." She accepted it between her fingers uncertainly. She tested its weight and texture, rolling it slightly between her fingertips.

"Give it a try."

With a hesitant glance at him, she brought it to her lips just as he had done. She puffed on it, inhaling. The taste of tobacco and a hint of something flowery filled her mouth. She pulled it away, working her lips and choking a little bit.

He grinned. "You should see your face."

"Blech." She shook her head.

"You don't have to like it."

She handed it back to him. "Curiosity satisfied, thank you very much."

"What else was on your agenda?"

"Um, let me think. I feel as though I've accomplished much, but now my agenda needs to be finding my friend."

It was troubling. Where could Olympia have disappeared to?

"She is a lone woman at Vauxhall after dark. Of course you're concerned."

She nodded and blew out a heavy breath. "That reminder does not help allay my fears."

Not that she was unaware of the dangers present for a lone woman anywhere at night. Evil hid in darkness, did it not?

The thing she had been telling herself all evening was how very capable Olympia was. She was wise beyond her years and discerning. It was as true as it was comforting. Olympia was not your standard girl.

She had a thirst for adventure and a way with people. She was adaptable, comfortable, and capable in many different settings. She would not stay in London forever. As much as it saddened Primrose to know Olympia would one day leave and move on, she admired her friend, and maybe envied her, too. Nothing intimidated Olympia.

Olympia had plans to see more of the world, a whole slew of destinations beckoned her. Norway, Switzerland, Russia. She wanted to see the Far East and Prim had no doubt she would.

If anyone could manage Vauxhall on her own, it was Olympia.

And yet Prim was still worried for her.

Amid the waning night, Prim began to wonder at what point

she should go home and see if Olympia had returned there looking for her.

That point, one could argue, had long since passed.

"I'm almost afraid to inquire the hour."

He reached inside his jacket for his pocket watch. "Nearing on two."

She exhaled. Nearing on two, and she had not stumbled on Olympia anywhere. Olympia could very well have assumed that Prim returned home. It would have been a reasonable expectation.

Nearing on two.

Whether or not she located Olympia, she would have to return home soon before the staff woke at dawn.

Their food arrived at the same moment the curtains lifted.

For a moment, she did not even notice what was happening on the stage. She fell on her food with ravenous focus. Tearing into the roasted pheasant with relish, taking special pleasure in the gooseberry sauce. Even the turnips, her least favorite vegetable, were a buttery, herbed delight on her tongue.

She moaned and then froze to find him watching her. Her mouth full, cheeks bulging with food, she brought her napkin to her lips with a smothered laugh.

He chuckled and then bit into a leg of pheasant, joining her in her gusto.

Their laughter faded away, the levity between them replaced with something else. His eyes moved over her, from her eyes and then to her lips.

Prim couldn't help herself. She looked to his mouth, too.

They were both remembering. Both back in that hedge. On that dark walk. Lost in each other's kisses.

Applause erupted and her attention was diverted, landing on the performance at the head of the theater.

"Um." She stopped and cleared her throat.

He cocked an eyebrow and then followed her glance to the stage. "Yes?"

"Those women . . ."

"Yes?"

"They . . . um. They're not wearing very many clothes."

"Yes. I believe the type of dancing they're doing is easier when not inhibited by skirts."

She nodded jerkily. "I—I can see that."

The women stood in a row, arms overlapping, connecting them as they danced in their bright stockings, kicking up their shapely legs in unison all the while singing. It was scandalous . . . and brilliant. Each dancer wore a different colored shoe with sparkly tassels.

Suddenly one dancer's shoe went flying, hitting somewhere near the front of the stage.

Prim squeaked out a laugh, clapping.

Jacob laughed, too. "Risks of the profession."

The women finished their dance and the curtains closed on them.

"Oh." She pouted as she clapped along with all the other wild applause.

"Fear not. They'll be back," Jacob assured her.

They continued eating. And talking. She did not think they'd ever run out of things to talk about, but of course they must stop soon. She would have to venture home after this.

The night must come to an end.

She didn't notice anything wrong at first. She merely thought the dancers had returned and that the audience was shouting out in approval.

She chased one of those surprisingly tasty turnips on her plate, glancing up occasionally to the stage, ready for more scandalous entertainment.

"Um, Prim?"

She looked at Jacob, instantly alarmed at the alertness of his expression. He rose slowly from the table, his hand stretching out toward her even though he wasn't looking at her. He was looking down toward the stage. She followed his gaze.

The dancers had not returned.

The curtains were still drawn . . . and flames were licking their way up them, the orange-gold tongues of fire eating the dark fabric.

For a moment, she could only stare, not grasping what she was seeing, vaguely thinking she was still watching some part of the show.

Then she made out all the shouts.

Fire! Fire! Fire!

Jacob caught hold of her hand then, pulling her up from her chair. "One of the stage lamps must have fallen over and lit the curtain on fire."

Pandemonium ensued.

They started down the small set of stairs to reach the bottom floor, but everyone was fleeing at once, congesting the stairs, bumping into each other in their panic to escape as the acrid smell of smoke rose in the air.

An elbow caught Prim in the cheek, and she cried out at the sharp explosion of pain in her face, her head jerking to the side. Heavens. She hoped she would not bruise as a result. She would have to invent a story if she did.

Jacob's hand tightened around hers and he tucked her closer to him.

When they finally reached the bottom floor it was no better. People were charging for the single door leading in and out of the theater.

Glass shattered nearby, and she flinched as the pungent scent of smoke thickened the air.

Someone pushed her from behind. She stumbled and managed to catch herself. If not for Jacob's hand holding hers, she would have gone down. But apparently Prim was still in the way. The person at her back took exception. He—or she—punched her.

She yelped as knuckles met with her spine. Her legs gave out as her body buckled from the impact.

"Prim!" Jacob turned, reaching for her, but then he was gone, torn from her, swept up in the swarm of bodies.

She heard him shout her name again, but she could no longer see him. She was lost in a sea of brightly colored gowns swirling around her as ladies fled in a growing haze of smoke.

She struggled to get back on her feet. Someone's slipper stomped on her fingers and a quick yelp escaped her again.

Suddenly she was lifted up. A hand grasped her arm and

dragged her forward. She shot a quick glance to an older gentleman.

"Thank you, sir!" she gasped and then succumbed to a fit of coughing.

He gave her a swift nod and released her arm, intent on his own escape.

She stayed on her feet, thankfully, her eyes tearing in the increasing smoke, as she moved along with the crowd through the door and out into the night, where it was chaos.

Bells clanged, signaling the fire brigade. Already several people were running toward the building with buckets of sloshing water.

She staggered, looking, searching through the sea of faces for Jacob. He was gone. Vanished. It was a melee. A mob of people gathered to gawk. Some to help. A few others were like her, looking for their own companions.

"Prim! Primrose!"

She swung around at the sound of her name.

Olympia charged toward her.

Prim went limp with relief at the sight of her.

Happy tears streamed down Olympia's face as she collided with Prim, locking her arms around her in a tight embrace.

"Where have you been? I've been looking for you everywhere." Olympia's hand cupped the back of her head as they hugged, holding her closely as though she feared Primrose might vanish from her arms.

Prim pulled back to look at her as she spoke. "I've been here . . . everywhere. Looking for you, too." She felt a tiny stab of guilt. She had been all over the Gardens on the pretense of searching for Olympia, but she knew she had not searched for her friend as well as she should have.

It was then that Prim noticed the person beside her friend— a tall, gangly young man.

Olympia followed her gaze. "Oh, this is Yani. He's a musician who has worked with my mother on several productions. He's been helping me search for you since we were separated at the tavern."

Yani bowed very properly before her. "Such a pleasure to find you well, Miss Ainsworth," he said over the din.

She nodded and then broke into a coughing fit.

Yani frowned and exchanged a worried look with Olympia.

Prim waved a hand in reassurance, regaining her breath. "I am well. I was able to escape before the smoke became too thick." She glanced back to the smoldering building, hoping no one was trapped inside. It seemed the fire brigade had matters in hand.

"You are certain you are well?" Olympia seized her hands and stepped back to look her over, her dark eyes narrowing as she examined her closely. "How did your gown get so filthy?"

"Er, yes. Sorry about that."

Olympia did not look heartened by her apology.

"Ladies, forgive me for interrupting, but things here are becoming a bit unruly. I suggest we take our leave."

Her heart jumped in her chest. Leave. *Without Jacob.*

But, of course, she couldn't keep him. Their destinies were not entwined beyond the arches of Vauxhall. She always knew they would have only tonight.

Still, Prim glanced wildly around. The tolling fire bell had not ceased. It rang out in jarring clangs on the night air.

A water brigade had formed, the line weaving like a snake through the crowd. Several people were screaming the names of people presumably lost or separated from them. One individual even had to be restrained from rushing back into the burning theater.

Uniformed watchmen appeared, ushering people toward the large archway, urging them to leave Vauxhall.

"Yes, come along, Prim." Olympia nodded. "I don't know about you, but I've had enough adventure for one night."

Prim moved along slowly, reluctantly, still craning for a glimpse of Jacob. She was confident he had left the building before her, forced out on a tidal wave of fleeing individuals, but she still wanted to see him one last time. To ensure he was he was unharmed. To say good-bye. To have that at the very least. A proper farewell.

"Prim! What's wrong? Make haste."

She snapped her attention back to Olympia and shook her head. "Nothing. I'm fine. Let us go."

She was not fine, but now was not the time to explain her night and share with Olympia all that had transpired, especially in front of Yani, who seemed perfectly nice, but was a veritable stranger.

Perhaps the time to confide in Olympia would never come. Perhaps this would be something she would keep to herself— something that was only hers, to be taken out and admired as a cherished heirloom.

A memory only for herself.

Prim followed Olympia and Yani toward the exit. Her friend kept a tight hold on her hand as though she feared they would be lost from each other again.

Prim moved hastily, forced to keep pace with them.

She risked several glances behind her even as they wound through the crowd, the hope of seeing him one last time fading . . . dying like a falling star.

Then he was there.

She spotted him in the distance, and the tight band squeezing around her heart eased and loosened. Countless bodies stood between them, including a line of people passing buckets of water.

He spotted her, too, his gaze skipping from Prim to Olympia, and some of the worry in his eyes dimmed. He'd been afraid for her—afraid she had been trapped in the burning building.

At least each of their fears were put to rest.

Everything stilled, grinding to a halt as nearly all sounds around her ceased to exist. Even the clanging bell was a dull, muted throb in her ears as they gazed at each other.

Olympia tugged on her. "Prim, come along."

She held up a hand, waving to him in farewell. It would have to be enough because it was all she would get. All she could give.

He lifted a hand, offering a wave in turn, and then he was gone, swept up in the crowd.

~~A dutiful daughter is the only kind worth having.~~
—*Lady Druthers's Guide to*
Perfect Deportment and Etiquette

The greatest duty is to oneself.

Chapter Fourteen

The sky was lightening to a bruised purple as Yani escorted them home to Belgrave Square. Prim didn't ask the time. She didn't have to. She knew it was close to the hour when the servants would begin stirring. Hopefully no one had woken too early or was a light sleeper.

Primrose sat silently in the carriage, speaking only when necessary to answer Olympia's questions. She stared out the crack in the curtained window, aware that she should be more nervous about sneaking back inside the house, but she could not summon forth the energy to worry. She was too preoccupied by the memory of Jacob waving good-bye to her. She didn't think she would ever forget that last glimpse of him.

She didn't want it to be good-bye, and yet she knew it was. She had known all along that it would end as abruptly as it began.

Yani brought them both to Olympia's house. He remained

in the carriage and then took his leave once they were safely deposited.

Prim hugged Olympia. "Thank you."

"For losing you?" Olympia snorted, patting her on the back.

"For being the best friend a girl could ask for."

Olympia squeezed her at those words. "You make it easy, Prim." They pulled apart, smiling at each other. "Next time we go to Vauxhall, let's actually go to Vauxhall. *Together.*"

Prim laughed. "Good idea." She darted across the deserted street then to her own house.

She was careful not to let the gate clang behind her. With a last wave for her friend, who stood watching at her own gate, she hurried to the servants' back door, aware that Cook would soon be up to start preparing breakfast for the day.

There were several stone pavers edging the small flower garden beside the back door. Prim located the one hiding the spare key and lifted it. Nothing. She simply stared at earth.

Frowning, she lifted another paver, assuming she had simply looked beneath the wrong one. Again, nothing but soil.

"Looking for this?"

Primrose gasped and looked up sharply. Losing her balance, she toppled onto her backside into the garden. At least this dress could not get anymore soiled.

Her mother stood framed in the doorway, brandishing a house key in her hand.

"Mama," she breathed.

"Primrose," she returned in a chillingly calm voice that matched her chillingly calm gaze.

Prim had never heard this voice from her mother before. She

would much rather have her shrieking and giving way to her histrionics. In other words, the mother she knew.

This mother terrified her.

"Inside," she directed Prim, the word dropping like a stone between them, sinking straight into Prim's stomach.

Mama turned and disappeared inside the house.

After a few moments and a bracing breath, Prim followed.

Primrose was not left alone in her room for long—just enough time to change out of her soiled borrowed gown into one of her simple frocks. She brushed her hair and pinned it back properly. Of course, she knew her mother would not forget the way Prim had looked when she opened that door and first clapped eyes on her, but presenting an image of a demure miss could not hurt.

Prim was pacing her chamber when her mother entered. Only her mother.

Prim peered over Mama's shoulder and glimpsed the empty corridor before she shut the door.

"Where is Papa?"

"You've sent him to his decanter of port in the library, where he's been since we discovered you gone."

"Oh." Disappointment lanced through her hotly. He was always the calm one. She had hoped he would be present during this first confrontation after her getting caught to help temper Mama's reaction.

Her mother moved into the room, walking in a deceptively easy stroll, no hint of unraveling into histrionics or a rage. Prim crossed her arms and tracked her movements nervously.

Mama's calm was especially misleading. When Prim looked

closely at her face, at the madly flaring tic near her right eye, she knew nothing calm resided in that woman. And those eyes . . . they looked wild—like a horse gone mad, ready to rear and kick its forelegs in the air.

Prim sank down on the edge of her bed, her arms still crossed. She had once shared this chamber with Aster, but when Begonia moved out, they no longer had to cohabit a room together. She had been glad for her own space—a bed of her own she could stretch out in. Except now Prim would do anything to have Aster here, in this room, with her now. Any buffer would have been much appreciated.

Prim tasted fear in her mouth. She didn't want to be alone with her mother. Cowardly, she supposed, but it was true.

It was not physical trauma she feared. Mama held all the power, and Prim was frightened of how she might choose to wield it over her. She'd rather face those footpads again from earlier. Goodness, she would prefer handing over her gown to Nell than enduring this.

She watched, unblinking, as Mama strolled to the window and parted the drapes to peer out at the square. Prim knew that view well. She knew that across the street loomed Olympia's stylish town house. Mama was looking directly at it.

Prim settled in deeper on the end of the bed, uncrossing her arms and folding her hands together in her lap. Never had she been around her mother for this long without a word being spoken.

After several more moments, Mama turned back around and approached, stopping several feet from the bed. She stared at Prim with those wild eyes, assessing in a way that felt probing and deep. It was unnerving. Mama had never given her such scrutiny before. "Pack your things."

Prim pulled back, confused. She opened and closed her mouth several times before saying, "I don't understand. What are you saying?"

"Pack. Your. Things. Make certain to bring all your warmer garments. It might be summer, but it gets chilly even in the day there."

Mama spoke so steadily, so matter-of-factly about sending her . . . somewhere.

About sending her *there*. Where was *there*?

Somewhere, apparently, where the weather ran cold, even in the summer months.

Mama lifted her chin in familiar hauteur. "You will go to stay with Aunt Bernice."

"Aunt Bernice lives in Yorkshire."

Her wild eyes flashed. "I'm aware of where my aunt lives."

"But you always said she lives in a Godforsaken village in a drafty old house with naught but two servants to attend to her—"

"She was left with a very small widow's portion and her only daughter married the local blacksmith. She has no one. No daughter to provide ease for her in her final years." Mama huffed. "Such a tragedy. My cousin should have considered her family and married well." Mama's eyes took on a decidedly vicious glint. "As a *good* daughter ought to do. Instead of self-ishly following her own desires." It was clear Mama was refer-ring to Prim. "Family ought to look after its own. Fortunately, I have a daughter to spare—one exceedingly troublesome and ungrateful daughter. *You*. I shall send you to care for her. *You* shall prove your worth and perhaps redeem yourself."

Primrose swallowed and blinked burning eyes. "But it is so very far away . . ." Her voice faded in a small tremble, pathetic even to her own ears. Far from London. From Olympia. Far from Aster. Even Papa she would miss—however much he didn't stand up for her. But then he never stood up for himself either. Or anyone. She could not fault him too much.

And she would be far from *him*.

Far from Jacob.

Absurd, she knew, to consider Jacob in this moment.

He should not even be on her mind. He was still a nob, and she was still Primrose Ainsworth. The gulf between them was wide. Prim being sent to Yorkshire should hardly signify.

No promises had been exchanged between them. No words vowing that they would see each other again. They had not even said a proper farewell.

Her adventure was over. In the past. And that's where Jacob would remain. She inhaled sharply. *At least you will have the memory of your night together to cherish and keep you warm during the long, cold Yorkshire nights . . . whilst he lives on in London, continuing his luxurious and fashionable life.*

Prim exhaled.

Mama continued, "You think that you deserve to go someplace better than Aunt Bernice's? After your behavior?"

"Must I *go* anywhere? Why can I not remain here? Why can you not punish me here?" It was what Mama had always done before when Prim displeased her.

"The last thing you need is to be anywhere you can get into

more trouble. Do you know what would have happened to this family if your shameful little outing had been discovered? You could have ruined us all. For all we know, it may yet still come to light. Perhaps you were seen?"

"I won't get into trouble again—"

"I cannot believe a word from your lips, and we cannot risk you staying here to stir up more of a mess."

"I was not discovered." Redding had not spotted her. At least she did not think so. She had worn a mask the majority of the time. Who else would have known her? As limited as her acquaintances were?

"No matter. You've proven you have a penchant for vice. You cannot be trusted."

Prim took a ragged breath. "How long must I live with Aunt Bernice?"

"You will stay with Aunt Bernice and be of comfort to her in her final years. However long that may be. God willing. Your sisters will be well settled by the time you come home. Papa and I will have had a nice respite too. Some much-needed peace—likely some lovely time together in Bath—before you come back."

Prim could not speak as she digested her mother's speech. She could only stare. Only withstand the ripples of shock reverberating through her.

She felt ill. As though she might lose the contents of her stomach all over her mother's slippers. Prim pressed a hand to her belly, waiting for the wave of nausea to subside.

When she finally recovered her voice, she managed to say, "Aunt Bernice is over"—she quickly calculated—"sixty years."

"Close to seventy, yes. I'm aware of her age."

"The women in our family live famously long lives."

"Yes. I'm aware we've been blessed with long age."

"What if . . ." Prim started haltingly, because she wouldn't wish her great-aunt's life to be shortened in any way. "What if she lives another ten years? Or longer? What if she lives to ninety? She very well could."

"Well, then you shall serve as a companion to her in her golden years."

"I could be near forty before I return home!"

"At that time, you would then return to care for me and Papa. My eyesight is already poor. I'm certain I shall need you to read to me."

She knew how Society worked. Marriage would be less of an option for a woman of forty. She would be deemed a spinster—thoroughly on the shelf and relegated to fetching drinks and shawls for her mother. She would be *that* daughter with no life of her own. Society was full of them. She would live out her life in service to her aging parents, and then when they were gone, she would have to rely on the kindness of her sisters to give her a home.

Someone please wake me from this nightmare.

While she did not feel driven to immediately marry, if she did not, she would then be stuck at the mercy of her family.

An altogether intolerable situation.

Marry a man and place yourself at his mercy, or remain forever at the mercy of your parents. Both, she realized, were intolerable.

Unless, of course, one married for love and affection. Unless one married someone one truly liked, someone who was a friend first.

Not that she had that option.

"Yes, well, you will stay with us. Let us face it, Primrose, you are not the manner of female a gentleman looks for as a wife."

It stung.

"So I will never have a season."

"I think it fair to dismiss that possibility altogether now."

"What of marrying me off? Has that not always been your goal?"

That was all her mother had ever talked about—getting her four daughters wed.

"You've proven tonight just how ineligible you are. Not every girl is suited to wifery. I'll not have you marry someone and then reveal just how poor a wife you are. I'll not endure that shame."

"You think so little of me that you would send me away over this one . . . blunder?"

Mama laughed harshly. "Blunder? You did not wear mismatched shoes or spill tea on your dress, Primrose. You, my girl, have always courted trouble. You are a scandal waiting to happen." Mama gave a single brusque nod. "Yes. You gone will make life so much easier."

You gone will make life so much easier. It stung.

When she didn't think her mother could do or say anything else to hurt her, that still managed to sting. It was a painful lesson to discover she was not quite as invulnerable as she thought.

Mama continued, "You must miss Violet's wedding, of course,

but naught to do about that. I will tell everyone Aunt Bernice was in urgent need of you. At any rate, I will breathe so much easier if I don't have you to worry about amid the festivities."

Prim sucked in a breath. Another blow.

"I'll not go," she announced, propping her hands on her hips.

Mama stilled. "I beg your pardon?"

"I will not go." Certainly, they would not send her against her will. Papa would not force her.

"Impudent chit. Who do you think you are?"

Prim lifted her chin much in the manner she had witnessed her mother do over the years. "I'm your daughter."

"Then be dutiful!" Mama slammed her fist in one open palm. Prim jerked from the force of it, as though she felt that blow on her body. "You've proven yourself unworthy. Make amends. And then after you've attended yourself most loyally to Aunt Bernice, you will come home to serve me as a companion in my dotage. You should be quite skilled at it after years of service to Aunt Bernice. That is your fate. In families with multiple daughters, it's not uncommon for one daughter to remain as a caretaker for the parents. You know this to be true, Primrose."

Indeed. She did know.

"You have it all planned out." Prim felt numb.

That is your fate.

It occurred to her that her mother had not arrived at this plan suddenly. She had not decided this tonight. Indeed not. Mama had been giving it some thought for a while now. She was far too ready with all the details. Perhaps it had been her plan all along. Or at least over the last year.

So this would be Prim's future.

She could not find the words to change Mama's mind. Nothing she said mattered. She wasn't being consulted. She wasn't being asked.

Mama nodded in satisfaction and moved toward the door. "You will see this is the best thing for you. For all of us. In time, you will thank me."

Her mother believed that.

Prim nodded rather than argue. It would not help.

Mama had decided her future.

Now Prim must decide what she could do to circumvent it. If there was a way in which she could still have a life of her own. Or was she well and truly without hope? Was all lost? As soon as her mother left, Prim rose from the bed and paced the chamber.

She would be leaving as soon as Mama made the arrangements. Mama would not want to waste time, in case there would be any consequences from tonight. That didn't give Prim much time to work out an alternative to the future Mama had planned for her. Perhaps she could be a governess. If she could convince Gertie to write her a recommendation . . .

She winced. Unlikely. Gertie lived in fear of Mama.

Perhaps Mrs. Zaher knew a family in need of a governess. She knew so very many people about Town, after all.

She winced again, considering her age. Governesses tended to be a bit older. Could she lie about such a thing without being found out?

Her head was spinning with so many wild ideas.

Her mind raced. *Olympia.*

Her very wise friend would provide insight. She needed to

talk to her. After that wretched exchange with her mother, Prim needed her friend. Olympia would settle her nerves and help Prim come up with a plan. Together, they could figure all this out. Breathing a bit easier, Prim moved to the door. Her hand closed on the latch and pulled, but was met with resistance.

She yanked on the latch. Jiggled it. Nothing.

The door didn't open.

She was locked in. A prisoner in her own home.

Prim snapped. Losing all composure, she banged on the door. "Unlock this door! You can't do this to me! Let me out!"

Nothing. No one came.

Of course they could do this to her.

She banged and kicked at the door for several more minutes until her toes ached. Until she was spent.

Wearied, she slid to the floor, leaning against the door for support.

She began to sob, pressing a hand flat to the door. "Please," she whimpered. "Don't do this."

She pressed a tear-soaked cheek to the wood.

"Prim," Aster whispered outside the door.

"Aster," she said anxiously, turning onto her knees, pressing both hands flat against the wood. "Aster, help me!"

"Shhh. Stop all the racket. It's not helping. You're angering Mama."

"What does it matter? She's sending me away."

"Violet is downstairs trying to persuade her against it."

She sniffed. "She is?" Violet was trying to help her?

"Yes, but cease all your wailing. It does you no good, only sets Mama more against you."

"Very well." She sniffed. "Thank you."

"We'll try to help."

"Thank you, Aster. And Violet. Thank her for me, too."

She heard her sister sigh through the door. "Oh Prim. Why did you sneak out? Was it worth it?"

Prim pressed her forehead flat against the door, thinking, considering her night. She played back everything that had transpired. The lush gardens of Vauxhall with their scents and sounds and sights. Not all good. Not all bad. But still . . . everything wondrous.

Jacob. The dark walk. The footpads. The kissing. *Jacob.* She'd talked more to him in one night than to anyone else in her house in years. She and Aster might get on together, but she was left alone so much of the time. The time she spent with Jacob had been a balm for her hungry soul.

She would not undo any of it.

"Yes," she whispered. "Yes. It was."

~~Trust in the guiding hand of your elders.~~
　　　　　—Lady Druthers's Guide to
　　　Perfect Deportment and Etiquette

*Use your own hand to guide
your fate.*

Chapter Fifteen

Prim was a prisoner.

A prisoner in her own home and in her own bedchamber. A prisoner in her head, in her thoughts and worries and misery.

A full day had passed since Mama locked her in her room, and no one had come to let her out. Gertie or the maid would bring her trays of food and take out her chamber pot. That was something to be grateful for, she supposed. Basic needs had become small blessings. She read from her books. Daydreamed about Jacob, playing over their conversations, their touches, their kisses.

Anything to stop herself from falling into the dark.

She often looked out the window, gazing across the street to Olympia's house, hoping to see her friend. She spotted Mrs. Zaher leaving once, but no other activity. Perhaps Olympia was in trouble, too. Prim felt awful for any difficulty she might have caused her friend.

On her second night locked away, the house was eerily silent. Or perhaps her isolation was starting to gnaw at her and chip away at her sanity. Dinner had been brought to her hours ago, and she felt certain everyone was in bed or out on the Town. She would not know. No one was apprising her of the comings and goings of the household occupants.

Prim tried to sleep. Except sleep would not come to her.

She was sprawled on her bed, staring at a crack in the plaster ceiling, when she heard a scratching against her door.

The sound of her name hissed through the wood. *"Primrose."*

Prim bounced up from the bed at her sister's voice. Dropping on her knees before her door, she pressed her hand flat to the cool panel of wood. "Aster?"

"Are you well?"

"How long are they going to keep me locked in here?" Her hand moved for the latch as though it might suddenly *not* be locked. As though her sister might have the power to free her.

"They're letting you out tomorrow. You're leaving for Aunt Bernice's in the morning."

The information rushed through Prim like a deluge of icy water.

She had hoped for more time. More time for a solution to come to her. More time for Aster or Violet to possibly sway Mama. More time for Papa to find his backbone and say no to Mama. More time for a miracle to happen.

She dropped her forehead against the door, fighting against a swell of defeat.

"We tried to convince her to let you stay through Violet's

wedding at the very least . . . but Mama doesn't care." Regret hummed in her sister's voice.

Aster continued, "I've tried talking to her. So has Violet. She can't be persuaded. I'm sorry, Prim. Perhaps Begonia can get through to her. I sent her a letter and told her what is happening. I'm certain she will pay a call soon."

Prim had not realized until now that she could count on all three of her sisters to be so loyal. It might be the one good thing to come out of this—discovering that her sisters supported her more than she would have guessed. All this time she had believed she was truly alone, but perhaps that was not the case. Perhaps she should have realized that sooner and reached out to them to bridge the gap.

Unfortunately, she would not be allowed to stay in London to appreciate this newfound realization.

Inexplicably, Jacob's face swam before her eyes.

She'd done her best to keep her thoughts away from him, but she had to admit to herself that she was grateful for their one night together more than ever.

She would have a sweet memory to comfort her in the long years ahead.

꧁꧂

The key scrabbled in the lock, sending Prim's heart into palpitations. Was it time? Had Mama come for her?

Prim had been working through possible plans of escape. Though none was very sound. All less-than-rational thinking she blamed on her forced isolation. If she remained locked away much longer, she'd be fit only for a cell in Bedlam.

She had dismissed jumping from her window. It was a long way down to the pebbled walk and definitely not a soft landing. She would not get very far with a broken leg. She had also considered barreling from her chamber the next time the door was opened. Although how far could she actually get? Legally, her parents were her guardians. She had no rights. They could ship her off to Yorkshire or force her to hard labor or send her to an Australian outpost. She was at their mercy.

Suddenly the door opened and Mama stood in the threshold. "Dress yourself."

Prim looked down at the very rumpled frock she had been lounging in. She lifted her chin in bravado. "If I'm to depart, I will be stuck in a coach traveling for hours. What does it matter what I wear?"

"You will not be departing today." Mama's lips closed in a shriveled-up pinch, as though her words tasted foul on her tongue. And yet she had uttered them. Hope fluttered inside Prim. She sat up a little straighter. "I won't?" Perhaps her sisters had persuaded Mama to change her mind after all.

"Don't look so hopeful. You're still going to Yorkshire. This is just a slight delay. You'll now depart tomorrow. Tonight, it seems, your presence is required."

Prim frowned. That made no sense. Her presence had never been needed anywhere before. Who required it? Certainly not Mama.

"Where am I . . . *required?*"

"Redding is having a small dinner party and has requested all of us attend."

"All of us? Even me?" That was strange.

"Yes. He was explicit that all of us attend. Even you." Mama's lips shriveled into that squished-up pinch again. "I can't imagine why."

Prim nodded in slow agreement. Neither could she. Redding had hosted several affairs since he began courting Violet. Never had Prim been included.

"I am bewildered." Mama fluttered a hand as though waving off a gnat. "I can only assume it is because his family has never met you. Perhaps his parents want to rectify that before the wedding. So be on your best behavior." She angled her head rather menacingly and wagged a finger at Prim. "I mean that, Primrose. I know it won't be easy, as you have proven yourself to be a hoyden time and time again."

"Or what?" She could not help the biting retort. "You're sending me away. What else can you do?"

"Don't challenge me, Primrose. There are always worse fates."

Staring at her mother's very determined and angry gaze, Prim realized this was true. She pressed her lips into a hard line and decided not to challenge her further. She gave a single nod of obedience.

Mama grunted in satisfaction. "I'll send Gertie around to help with that nest you call hair."

With that said, she was gone and Primrose was left alone again. Alone, but with the full knowledge that she would be free one last night before she was shipped off and forgotten.

It was not a small dinner party. Not by any definition.

It was more. Much more. Make no mistake.

The large house was bursting at the seams with people. Prim

supposed it could be defined as a dinner party in the strictest sense of the term, as there was food to be had. But there were so many guests, they ate in rotations in the grand dining room, called in by liveried grooms and seated very obviously according to rank. It was the kind of thing Prim had read about in Lady Druthers's book. She'd heard her sisters talk about such things.

This was a ball. Unequivocally.

The sheer number of guests eliminated it from being ruled as anything as small or intimate as the dinner party she had been expecting. And there was dancing to the strains of a full orchestra positioned in the corner of the large marble-parquet ballroom—a ballroom Prim's entire house could have fit inside.

She looked around her in wonder. This was to be her sister's life. Prim knew Violet was marrying into a wealthy family, but she had not truly *known*. She had not seen the evidence with her own eyes before tonight. Of course, she still did not approve of the method in which Redding's family earned its wealth. She remembered Jacob's words then, suggesting that she might be able to influence Redding.

She doubted that would be possible given her future exile to Yorkshire. Perhaps if she were remaining here, she could have made a difference in time.

Mama was livid, of course. Papa was lost in one of the card rooms and did not seem inclined to care when there was such diversion to be had. Mama frequently glanced Prim's way as though she were somehow responsible for disrupting her plans. As though Prim had somehow orchestrated her invitation from her locked bedchamber.

"I do not understand," Mama muttered to Violet. "Why did Redding not make it clear this was no simple dinner party?" She looked down at her elegant dress. "I would have worn a different gown."

Prim did not know what Mama was complaining about. Primrose looked down and frowned at her own gown. It was hopelessly dated and childish and frayed from use along the seams. Mama had refused to let Prim borrow one of her sisters' more mature and sophisticated gowns in what was clearly a flash of pique. Primrose might be allowed to attend this evening, but by God she would look like a poor relation.

Mama was still talking. ". . . and I would not have brought Primrose along had I known. I don't care what Redding said. Why did he insist on Primrose's presence?"

Violet shrugged in that unhelpful way of hers. Her gaze scanned the room, the expression mild on her beautiful face. "I do not know. You always tell me not to pester him with trifling questions—"

"Oh! This is not trifling! This is important! This is very important, Violet." Mama bobbed her head fiercely.

"Mama," Aster whispered. "People are staring."

Their mother's face reddened as she glanced around to discover several people looking their way. If there was one thing Mama hated, it was a spectacle. To clarify, she enjoyed observing spectacles . . . as long as they did not involve her.

"Well," she said, her voice much more subdued. "This is vastly improper. Primrose should not be here."

Aster tried for calm. "He explicitly invited her."

"Yes. And why is that?" Mama stabbed her fan in Prim's

215

direction. "Why should he care one whit on the matter of your sister's attendance this evening?" She looked suspiciously at Violet. "Is this your doing? To delay me sending your sister away? It won't work. She leaves tomorrow."

"It was not me," Violet said defensively. "Although what difference will one day make?" Violet rolled her eyes, waving in the general direction of her betrothed. "I haven't the foggiest notion. If you really must know, why don't you go march over there and ask him yourself, Mama?"

That was a challenge their mother certainly would not accept. And Violet knew that.

Mama puffed up like a bird with riled feathers. "Well, I would never . . ."

"Then please, for the love of all that is holy, cease haranguing me on the matter."

"Hmpf" was Mama's only response.

"Oh, I see dear Felicity. I must go say hello." Violet slipped away with a relieved exhalation and Primrose envied her easy escape.

Mama whipped her glare to Aster.

Aster shrugged.

"What are you doing standing here on the fringe of the ballroom? You should be out there socializing and winning yourself some admirers." She fluttered her hand at the dense crowd.

Despite Mama's rebuke, Aster did not move to follow her bidding. If anything, her sister shrank back further.

Mama shook her head in disgust then turned her gaze on Prim.

It was unfortunate timing, for Prim was caught sending a glance of longing to the colorful swirl of dancing figures.

Mama scowled, her countenance turning particularly spiteful. "Do not look so pleased with yourself," she admonished.

Prim could not help it. She was released from the prison of her room and out in Society. It was finally happening. She had thought she would be stuffed into a carriage this day and on her way north. Instead she was at a ball. It might be the only ball she would attend in the next couple of decades, but here she was, nonetheless. She would not pretend to dislike it.

It also amused her to think that Mama had been forced into this—into doing something she would have never done under normal circumstances. Aster's warning about keeping her voice down must have had some influence, however. Mama glanced around warily and leaned closer to mouth something at Primrose that she could not even begin to interpret. The words were much too angry and flying much too quickly from her lips.

Then Mama stopped. Froze. Her eyes bulged as she fixed on something just beyond Prim's shoulder.

The tiny hairs at the back of Prim's neck tingled in awareness. Her stomach churned uneasily.

Slowly, Prim turned. Redding stopped before them. Her gaze skipped right over him, however, to the man beside him.

Jacob. He was here, standing before her.

The din of the ballroom faded. Prim could scarcely hear Redding speaking even as she recognized that his lips were moving. His words were dim and far away, as if coming from within a cave.

"Mrs. Ainsworth, Miss Aster, and Miss Primrose, allow me to introduce my guest this evening, the Duke of Hampstead."

Primrose could not move.

The Duke of Hampstead.

It could not be true.

It could not be . . . Jacob. He would have said. They spent an entire night together and he would have said if he was a blasted duke! That would be the kind of thing one mentioned.

Jacob's dark eyes watched her with familiar intensity, and she knew he was gauging her reaction and properly reading her astonishment.

Prim was aware of a few things happening around her: a general murmur that carried throughout the room in an undulating current, her sister and mother performing hasty curtsies. Prim found she could not do the same. She could not offer the expected courtesy. She had turned into a hunk of marble, lost in Jacob's familiar stare.

Familiar and yet oddly strange here, in the surplus of candlelight glowing throughout the ballroom.

His gaze was trained on her. He did not even glance at her mother or sister. Only Prim.

He looked only at her.

Redding was still speaking. Mama uttered something perfectly inane.

Primrose heard her name and turned slowly to see her mother sending her killing glares.

"I said, would you go fetch my shawl, Primrose dear? I am quite cold." She asked the question between her teeth. The evening was as warm as any summer evening. She clearly wanted Prim gone from the sphere of a duke.

Prim nodded, but did not move or speak. It was all too impossible, too astonishing.

Mama was gesturing to Aster. "My daughter, Aster, is a beautiful dancer, Your Grace. Why, Mrs. Beckworth herself said she had not seen so graceful a girl at Almacks in many a season."

Not that they were of a class to frequent Almacks, but Mama liked to make it sound as though they did. The Ainsworths had never received an invitation to any assembly there, but Mrs. Beckworth had. Mama had made that particularly grand lady's acquaintance once, and once was all it took for Mama to invent all manner of exchanges between Mrs. Beckworth and herself. All fabrication, of course, because no one would ever claim Aster to be a beautiful dancer.

"Is that so?" Jacob murmured, still scrutinizing Primrose.

Mama followed his gaze to Prim with a perplexed frown.

"Ah, Prim?" Mama said tightly. "My shawl?"

Mama could be no more direct. She wanted Prim gone from them.

Just then the orchestra struck up a waltz.

"Ah! Lovely. The first waltz of the night," Mama proclaimed, giving Aster a hard elbow, nudging her forward.

Jacob took one stride forward.

Mama's face lit up and then fell to confusion as he bowed before Primrose and took her gloved hand in his.

"Miss Ainsworth. Might I have this dance?"

~~Do not let the selfish and greedy pursuit of happiness prevent you from living your most modest and correct life.~~

—*Lady Druthers's Guide to*
Perfect Deportment and Etiquette

Happiness matters.

Chapter Sixteen

Jacob's eyes glinted at Primrose over her hand, and she knew he was immensely enjoying himself in this moment. Lifting it up, still clasping her fingertips, he turned to look at her gaping mother. "With your permission, of course, Mrs. Ainsworth."

"I—I—" Her mother's mouth sagged open, revealing its inside. It was most unappealing.

She sputtered for a few more moments until finally Aster piped up beside her. "Of course. Mama would be happy for you both to take a turn about the floor." Aster's gaze swung back and forth between Mama and Primrose.

Mama was still unable to speak. A miracle in and of itself. Prim would have to mark this date for posterity.

Jacob's gaze fastened on Prim's face. "Miss Primrose?"

"Yes. Yes, I should like that, Your Grace."

Without waiting for her mother to collect herself and manage a response, Jacob led Prim out onto the dance floor.

As soon as they were standing in the center of the marbled parquet, they settled into the proper position—one of her hands clasped in his, the other on his very solid shoulder.

The duke's broad hand settled on the small of her back, bringing her in close, and she was assailed with the scent of him and the memory of them together. She closed her eyes briefly. *Don't swoon.*

They began waltzing, joining the other couples whirling around them.

"What are you doing here?"

"Delivering on that waltz I promised you."

He remembered that?

"This is madness," she whispered, feeling the multitude of stares on them. It was a wholly new sensation to find herself the subject of so much attention.

People were staring, and Mama was dead somewhere in the ferns edging the ballroom.

She would have enjoyed that if this was not all so mortifying.

"A promise is a promise."

She started to shake her head and then stopped herself. She was dancing with a duke. This was not the time to look dis-agreeable and make people wonder. At least no more than they already were.

"How did you even know I would be here?"

He smiled down at her. "How do you think *you* even find yourself here?"

She digested that question and then it dawned on her. The reason she had been invited here tonight, why Redding had insisted she come . . .

"*You.* You did this."

He nodded once, looking supremely satisfied with himself.

"You," she continued, "are the reason I was invited to this ball?"

"I," he clarified, "am the reason Redding even had this ball on such short notice. It was originally a small dinner party."

"Redding knows about you and me?" Her voice faded at her utterance, as it conceded so much, namely that there existed a *them.* An arrogant assumption. After only one night together, there was no *you and me.*

"He merely knows that I'm an admirer of yours. Not any of the particulars of how I came to be your admirer."

She turned that over in her head. Of course Redding would not question him. He would just be thrilled to have the Duke of Hampstead in his home.

Prim sent a quick glance around them, noting all the stares, and not particularly liking them. She couldn't help thinking that the ladies were all laughing at her behind their fans. They probably thought it a jest that she was waltzing with the celestial young duke. And the dratted dress, so homely and out of style. That would be dissected in detail in tomorrow's scandal rags.

"This is all too much," she murmured, and then gasped as he spun her around.

"Enjoy your waltz and stop fretting," he chastised lightly.

"I am . . . trying . . ."

And she did try, except every now and then she would search for and locate her mother—and she would see her shocked and bewildered face. She was probably afraid that Primrose would say or do something that would plunge their entire family into shame and ruin them into the next century.

"Prim?" She looked up into his compelling eyes at the sound of her name, and it felt like their night in Vauxhall all over again, when it had been just the two of them. Gazing at his face, she could almost forget everything else.

"You found me," she whispered, recalling their farewell waves. She had thought that was the end, the last time she would ever see him.

"Did you think I would not? How could I forget you? You're the first person I've been myself with in . . ." He blew out a breath. "Perhaps ever."

"You did not tell me you were the Duke of Hampstead."

"And you did not tell me you're Miss Ainsworth."

She made a face at him. "It's not the same thing and you know it." Compared to him, the Ainsworths were chimney sweepers.

He inclined his head in acknowledgment. "I know I should have, but it felt so bloody *good* to be with someone who wasn't with me because of my title."

She exhaled, refusing to let giddy delight overtake her. Her life was complicated. Too complicated for him to make her feel happy right now. "I'm being sent away," she announced.

He frowned. "What do you mean?"

"I was caught returning home from Vauxhall the other night. Er, the other morning. My family knows I snuck out and now I'm being sent away."

"For how long?"

"For the foreseeable future. I'm off to Yorkshire to live with my aunt."

"No." He was quick to rebut.

"It is decided."

"No. It won't happen."

"I'm afraid it is happening. The arrangements have already been—"

"Not after tonight."

"What do you mean?"

"Well, after tonight it will become clear I'm courting you. I am your suitor now."

She stumbled, and he caught her, pulling her closer and sweeping her along, his hand splayed wide at her back. She was certain she would feel the warm imprint of his hand long after he removed it.

I'm your suitor now.

Such a declaration was audacious and presumptuous . . . and mad. But also thrilling. She could not deny that her heart was suddenly lodged somewhere in the vicinity of her throat.

He continued, "Your mother would be foolish to send you away now, and while I do not know her, I doubt she is a fool."

She fought to swallow so that she could answer. "No. No, she is no fool." She was other things. *Many* other things, but not a fool.

If a duke was courting any one of her daughters, Mama would certainly not send that daughter to rusticate in the countryside. That flew in the face of everything Mama wanted out of life: rank, esteem, recognition, and invitations to every coveted event in Society. No hostess would leave the mother of the girl a duke was courting off her guest list.

Prim's gaze once again sought out her mother, finding her

standing with all three of Prim's sisters. Begonia, Violet, and Aster had joined Mama's side to join in the gawking.

It did not stop with Prim's sisters, however. A whole entourage of ladies clustered around Mama—ladies who had snubbed Mama earlier in the night . . . and other times. Suddenly they now found her worthy of their company.

Even Olympia was there. She must have just arrived. Prim felt a rush of happy relief at the sight of her friend. She had worried about her, hoping she was not in trouble in any way from their night out.

Olympia sidled close to Aster and the two of them bent their heads together in conversation. No doubt Aster was catching her up on all that had transpired. An easy smile curved Aster's lips and Prim realized it was the first genuine smile from her all night. Prim's glance swept over them, pausing at the sight of their gloved hands. Their fingers intertwined subtly for a brief moment and their eyes held—locked in a warm and intimate manner.

Prim pulled her attention from her best friend and sister to her mother. Mama no longer looked so bewildered. She was a vision of delighted wonder, her hands clasped together as her gaze tracked Prim and Jacob.

"You don't need to do this," she hissed at Jacob.

"Do what?"

"Save me. Again," she added, thinking about how he'd rescued her from being trampled in that brawl in the tavern and later from the footpads in the dark walk.

"As I recall, we saved each other—multiple times—but in any case, that is not what I am doing here."

"No?"

"No."

She sniffed, hardly mollified. She did not believe him.

Things like this did not happen in real life.

Now that she knew Jacob was the Duke of Hampstead, all the rumors she had heard about him came flooding back.

Jacob did not do things like this.

Respectable *ton* parties bored him. He was a perpetual bachelor, uninterested in courtship, by all accounts. He shied away from all the festivities the *ton* had to offer, never even stepping foot inside Almacks, where the most celebrated debutantes assembled to be plucked off the marriage mart accordingly.

And he wants to court me?

It was madness.

She gave her head a small shake. She did not qualify as good *ton*. Papa was a gentleman, but that was the highest designation that could be applied. It could be argued that the Ainsworths were not even quality gentry, and Jacob was nobility.

He was here for her out of pity or obligation . . . and she would not have it.

Prim couldn't help but feel that the wonderful time they'd had together at Vauxhall was somehow tainted now.

She did not need his pity.

As the waltz wound down to its last chords, Prim extricated herself from Jacob's, *no*, Lord Hampstead's arms. A bit hasty, but nothing eyebrow raising. No one could say she *fled* his arms . . . precisely.

Nevertheless, he noted her rush to be free of him and he

frowned as he bowed before her. She, in turn, dipped into a curtsey, her earlier paralysis forgotten.

Her first curtsey, she realized, in public. And her first waltz, too. With a much-fêted duke. She was well and truly out in Society now whether Mama liked it or not. It could not be stopped. Prim could not be stuffed back into the cage at this point.

Dear heavens. She glanced around. Every single gaze was turned on her. He'd made her. Solidified her place as a Person of Interest in Society. She could already feel it. Things were different now. The stares and whispers directed her way signified that.

The duke took her hand and bestowed a lingering kiss to the back of her glove. "Did I mention you look lovely tonight?"

She smirked. "In this frock?" She had been the subject of titters and laughter upon arriving. Her dress was hopelessly childish.

"I am quite convinced, Miss Primrose, you would look lovely in a burlap sack."

Her face caught fire. "You are too generous with your flattery, Your Grace."

His smile slipped slightly. He leaned forward just an inch closer. Not so much as to be inappropriate, but enough to make her heart race. "I miss the sound of my name on your lips."

Now her heart was pounding against her ribs, ready to burst free. "Well, you've kept your promise. Thank you for the waltz. Now, please ask someone else to dance. Perhaps then no one will think you are singling me alone out."

They'd danced. They were finished.

"But I *am* singling you out."

She shook her head once and forced a brittle smile. "You should not say such things to me." Such very tempting things that made her wish for the impossible.

He shook his head. "I intend to claim the next waltz of the evening."

Her eyes went wide. "You cannot. Everyone would think . . ." Her voice faded.

"That the Duke of Hampstead is completely besotted?"

Dumbfounded, she nodded.

He leaned forward. "And that would be true."

It could not be . . . real. *Could it?*

At least there would not be another waltz for a while. She took solace in that. They would not play them back-to-back. She might be new to balls, but she was well versed in the rules of Society.

"I don't . . ."

"Understand. Clearly." Smiling slightly, he shook his head as if she were a marvel. "Did you think I was just going to forget about the girl I spent the night with at Vauxhall?"

She nodded mutely.

He smiled almost tenderly. "Oh no. That girl and I are going to be spending a lot more time together."

"But people will think . . ."

"And they will be right, Primrose Ainsworth. You've landed yourself a duke." A look of uncertainty crossed his face. "If you want him."

She hesitated, moistening her lips. "I don't care about landing a duke." That had never been her dream. "I do care . . . about you. About being with you."

The uncertainty vanished from his face and he grinned then, looking suddenly boyish.

The orchestra at that moment started another waltz.

Before she knew it, she was swept up in Jacob's arms for the second time this evening.

"Another waltz so soon?" she asked breathlessly.

Whispers ran along the edges of the ballroom like wildfire.

"The perks of being a duke. I had Redding arrange it. I wanted to make the most of our waltz."

Waltzes. "People will talk. They will think you besotted—"

"With you? I am, and I'm happy for them to think so."

Her mouth closed with a snap. She was silent for several moments as they danced, digesting that.

Some of the tension ebbed from her shoulders. Suddenly she no longer cared about the stares and whispers around them. She felt . . . happy. She felt free.

Most of all, she felt hopeful.

He'd done all this. He'd arranged all this—this entire night. For her.

This wasn't pity or obligation.

He had wanted to see her.

He wanted to court her.

He wanted to *more* than court her.

"Yes," she finally said with a true smile, nothing fake or brittle about it, stretching her lips.

He smiled back and teased, "Now, how would you feel about sneaking off onto a dark balcony with me?"

A giggle slipped free. "That sounds like very compromising

behavior, and we're already toeing the line of scandal as it is. With all eyes on us tonight, we would certainly be caught."

Mama would likely be out there in the first five seconds, an army of witnesses in tow. Regarding *this* scandal, she'd be thrilled—whatever it took to get her daughter to the altar with a duke.

"Would that be so terrible?" he asked.

"To be caught in a compromising position? Er, that would prove awkward. We would not be courting anymore. We would be betrothed." She giggled again, only this time she felt a touch nervous uttering the b-word out loud.

Honor would demand he offer for her in such a scenario, and Jacob was an honorable man.

"Would that be so terrible?" he repeated and her heart squeezed.

Her smile slipped away and she looked at him in seriousness. "I would not want to marry anyone because the rules of Society demanded it." As far as she was concerned, that was never a reason.

He sobered then, his smile fading. "I can promise you this. I would never feel *forced* into marrying you, Primrose. It's something I'd gladly do, but you're correct. All jesting aside, scandal should not be the thing that brings us together."

The waltz ended. With a wink, he settled her hand in the crook of his elbow. Together, they exited the dance floor and faced the world.

~~Do not fool yourself. Courtship is a battlefield,~~
~~fraught with foes you must defeat.~~
~~You must win or perish.~~

—Lady Druthers's Guide to
Perfect Deportment and Etiquette

Love.

Epilogue

Three hundred and sixty-two days later . . .

Primrose's family and friends disembarked from the boat onto the dock with happy exclamations. Even Mama appeared flush with excitement, with tiny beads of perspiration dotting her forehead as they faced the wonder of Vauxhall Gardens, a place she had never deigned to visit before, but at Jacob's suggestion she'd declared the notion providential.

"This way," Jacob directed.

When he had announced that he wanted to take them all to the pleasure gardens to celebrate Prim's birthday, Prim had looked to Mama, ready for her objections. Prim should have known better.

Of course Mama would have forgotten her reservations about visiting Vauxhall. Or maybe it was simply that she agreed to anything the Duke of Hampstead proposed as long as he continued to court her daughter.

Jacob could have suggested that they visit a Seven Dials bordello to mark the occasion of Prim's birthday and Mama would have likely agreed.

They all trekked up the hill to the grand stone arch entrance, their large party spilling into the Gardens, to where Prim had absconded to celebrate her birthday a year ago.

Jacob had vowed there would be no skipping Prim's birthday

this year. According to him, they would celebrate it in grand fashion this year and every year.

At his invitation, everyone had joined them. Mama and Papa. Olympia. Violet and Redding. Begonia with her family. Aster. They could not wait to see what the young duke had in store for them all.

Prim could hardly wait herself. She glanced at the faces of her family, wondering who was most excited. It was difficult to discern. Everyone looked so very pleased as they descended on the revelry of Vauxhall with the young duke for escort.

Mama had never been so agreeable. She was kind to all, reveling in the coup of her family's connection to the Duke of Hampstead. She had even let go of her obsession to see Aster wed.

Aster appeared quite satisfied with the transformation that had come over Mama. She was perfectly content with her unattached status. She glowed as she walked closely beside Olympia this evening. The two of them had become inseparable this past year, a deep friendship blooming between them.

Olympia accidently dropped her reticule as they walked and Aster quickly retrieved it for her, returning it to her with a tender smile. Olympia blushed, her cheeks pinkening charmingly.

"Here we are," Jacob declared as they arrived to a covered courtyard that overlooked the river.

An orchestra was set up, already playing on a dais. Several jugglers and clowns and fire-eating acrobats wove through an arrangement of linen-draped tables. A man with a large, brightly feathered bird stood at the edge, prompting the lovely creature to spout Lord Byron's "She Walks in Beauty."

"A parrot reciting poetry," Papa marveled.

Mama fanned herself, her eyes agog as she no doubt quickly calculated the cost of such extravagance.

Prim's nieces squealed in delight and rushed from Begonia's side.

Liveried servers stood at the ready, holding trays of drink and standing beside the ornate silver service keeping their lunch warm. The aroma of enticing foods laced the air, mingling with all the many rich smells of Vauxhall.

Her brothers-in-law quickly made their way to the champagne.

"You did this for me?" she breathed, her chest swelling with what was now becoming familiar joy. Her life this last year had been fraught with one delight after another. She was free from her stifling box and never going back.

Jacob leaned close, his lips brushing her ear as he spoke. "Happy birthday, Prim."

Fall in **love** with a great book!

HMH teen

Find Your Story

New York Times Best-Selling Author
SOPHIE JORDAN
SIXTEEN SCANDALS

Sometimes looking back is the only way to move forward.
SOME OTHER NOW
SARAH EVERETT

Under Shifting Stars
ALEXANDRA LATOS

a love story in bloom
things that grow
Meredith Goldstein

chemistry lessons
Meredith Goldstein

MARI'S DAD IS RUNNING.
MARI IS RISING.
RUNNING
NATALIA SYLVESTER

HMH teen